"Shanna, we go...
the prints at th...
the lab technician said.

"Who is it?" she asked eagerly, glancing at Quinn beside her. An identity would get them one step closer to finding the killer.

"This is going to be a bit of a shock," the technician continued. "We have a set of fingerprints matching a child who's been missing for fourteen years."

A child? Missing for fourteen years? No. Oh, no. Her stomach twisted. She grabbed the edge of the doorframe for support. "Who?"

"Your sister. Skylar Dawson."

Skylar. It was Shanna's fault her little sister had been kidnapped fourteen years ago. Her fault that her parents had divorced, destroying what was left of their family. After fourteen years of not knowing anything, those fingerprints meant that Skylar was alive!

But her sister's prints were found at the crime scene, which made her one of the many suspects in Quinn's half brother's death.

Books by Laura Scott

Love Inspired Suspense

The Thanksgiving Target
Secret Agent Father
The Christmas Rescue
Lawman-in-Charge
Proof of Life

LAURA SCOTT

grew up reading faith-based romance books by Grace Livingston Hill, but as much as she loved the stories, she longed for a bit more mystery and suspense. She is honored to write for the Love Inspired Suspense line, where a reader can find a heartwarming journey of faith amid the thrilling danger.

Laura lives with her husband of twenty-five years and has two children, a daughter and a son, who are both in college. She works as a critical-care nurse during the day at a large level-one trauma center in Milwaukee, Wisconsin, and spends her spare time writing romance.

Please visit Laura at www.laurascottbooks.com, as she loves to hear from her readers.

Proof
of Life

Laura Scott

Love Inspired

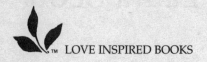

Recycling programs
for this product may
not exist in your area.

LOVE INSPIRED BOOKS

ISBN-13: 978-0-373-67486-2

PROOF OF LIFE

www.LoveInspiredBooks.com

Printed in U.S.A.

Give thanks to the Lord for He is good;
His love endures forever.
—1 *Chronicles* 16:34

This book is dedicated with love to my son Jon.
I hope you know how proud I am of the
kind and generous young man you've become.

ONE

Crime-scene investigator Shanna Dawson paused on the threshold to gather her bearings. The dilapidated four-room house reeked of stale beer, cigarette smoke, greasy fast food and the rancid horror of death. As a CSI, she was more accustomed to the latter than the former.

The interior of the house, located a few blocks from Carlyle University, a private college outside of Chicago, was a pigsty; fast-food containers, smelly clothes, dirty dishes and empty beer cans were strewn everywhere. Talk about a CSI's nightmare.

For a moment she imagined the kids who lived there. The victim, Brady Wallace, was a young college student who shared the place with three other guys. Yet despite the mess, she imagined this was the type of place the so-called popular kids would gravitate to for parties. A college student's version of fun and excitement.

Not hers, though. During her four years of college she'd never been invited to student gatherings. The party scene had never appealed to her. She was too serious, too introspective to indulge in lighthearted activities.

Fun hadn't been a part of her world in a long time.

Suppressing a sigh, she got to work. There was so much evidence to collect, she'd easily be here for hours. As she walked through the foyer and into the living room, she overheard two cops arguing.

"This is a homicide investigation, Murphy. Campus police don't have jurisdiction over homicides."

"I know. But this incident occurred on my turf. Give me a break, Nelson. The victim is my brother."

"Half brother," the detective corrected.

"Brother just the same." The campus cop, Murphy, was stubborn. After a long moment where it seemed the homicide cop wasn't going to give in, Murphy sighed and scrubbed a hand along his bristly jaw. "At least give me the courtesy of keeping me informed of the details of your investigation."

Murphy snagged her attention, mostly because he was the victim's half brother and because he didn't look much like the local campus cops she was used to. And not just because of his tall, broad-shouldered good looks. His body appeared to be pure muscle, and he wore his wheat-blond hair military short. His face wasn't handsome in the traditional sense but bore deeply worn grooves of experience, as if he'd carried the weight of the world on his shoulders. His green eyes held the shadows of a deep pain she could relate to. She was inexplicably drawn to him, as if he might be a kindred soul, but she forced herself to turn away, examining the crime scene.

Brady Wallace's body was lying on the floor, in the walkway between the living room and the kitchen. His bright red hair was matted with blood, the left side of his skull concave where it had been crushed. A heavy marble rugby trophy was lying on the floor beside him, the four-by-four-inch base covered with hair and blood. She imagined microscopic evidence would confirm the blood and tissue matched the victim's scalp.

The position of the body was distinctive. Why was he lying on the floor, in the walkway between the living room and kitchen? Had he run from his attacker? Or had he been on his way to the kitchen for something to eat when someone clubbed him from behind?

And who could hate a college student enough to kill him?

Brady was young, barely twenty. The callous waste of a young life always upset her. She'd grown up believing in God, but over the years had drifted away from the church and her faith. And at times like this, when she faced the hard edge of death, she really couldn't understand God's plan. What had this kid done to deserve death? She couldn't imagine. Feeling slightly sick, she glanced back over at the two cops who'd fallen silent as they'd registered her presence. She forced a professional expression on her face as she faced their curious stares. "Who found the body?"

"One of his roommates, Kyle Ryker." Murphy's face was bleak as he scanned the room. "Four boys live here—the victim, Brady Wallace, and three others—Kyle Ryker, Dennis Green and Mark Pickard."

"They must have had a party last night," she murmured with a wry sigh. Saturday nights were big party nights, so she shouldn't be surprised. "I'd hate to think the place always looks like this."

Murphy grimaced and lifted a shoulder. "It's not much better on any other day. But you're right—they did have a party, one that apparently lasted until the wee hours of the morning. According to Kyle, Brady was alive at four in the morning, when Kyle went upstairs to crash for what was left of the night. When Kyle came down to get something to eat from the kitchen about nine-thirty, he tripped over Brady's body."

As Brady's half brother, Murphy obviously had a personal stake in solving this crime. She felt a tug of sympathy. She knew better than anyone how difficult it was to deal with the violent aftermath of a crime that hit too close to home.

"I'm Detective Hank Nelson." The older cop, wearing the ill-fitting polyester suit coat, quickly introduced himself. "And this is University Campus Police Officer Quinn Murphy. I'll be taking the lead on this homicide investigation."

She understood the implied order and gave both men a brief nod. "Shanna Dawson, crime-scene investigator. My boss, Eric Turner, will be joining me shortly. If you gentlemen wouldn't mind stepping outside, I'd like to get to work."

The two cops exchanged a long look as if debating their right to stay, but in the end they both turned and headed for the door.

"Officer Murphy?" she called, before they could both disappear.

He turned toward her, his eyebrow raised questioningly. "Yes?"

"I'd like to talk to you later, if you have time." She knew Detective Hank Nelson would do the full investigation into all aspects of Brady's life, but she was curious to know more about Brady. Her methods might be somewhat unorthodox, but the more she understood the victim, the better job she'd do with her investigation. As the victim's brother, Murphy would be a great source of information.

"Of course." He came over to hand her his campus police business card. "Call me when you're finished processing things here."

"I will." She pocketed the card and watched him leave. When she was alone, she picked up the camera around her neck and began to record the initial evidence of the crime scene.

Quinn Murphy would mourn his half brother's passing, but at least he had the comfort of knowing what happened. Maybe not the who or the why, but the rest. All some families knew was that a loved one had disappeared. They never knew if their loved one was dead or alive, at peace or living in some awful situation, praying for salvation and longing for home.

Shanna took a deep breath and let it out slowly, shaking off the painful memories of the past. She'd made it her mission over the years to bring families closure. To bring the comfort of knowledge. The peace of acceptance. Today she'd collect every possible clue, piece together as much of the puzzle as she could until she discovered who killed Brady Wallace and why. She'd do whatever was possible to help Brady's family begin to heal.

Even though there were many wounds that never could.

"It's going to take us forever to dust for prints," her boss pointed out in exasperation. "The kids had a party on Saturday night, and there were probably at least fifty people in and out of this place. How on earth are we going to isolate anything useful?"

Eric was right—this was a long shot for sure. "The police are interviewing the roommates, trying to get a list of party attendees together. I believe this is personal, likely someone with a grudge against Brady." She glanced around the filthy room, imagining how the events might have played out. "I have a hunch this kid knew his attacker. To have this happen after a party doesn't come across as premeditated, but more like a crime of opportunity, as if Brady was in the wrong place at the wrong time. Using the trophy to bash in his head could have been a simple act of rage or revenge. I'd like to start by dusting Brady's bedroom and the living room for prints."

Eric let out another sigh. "It just seems like a lot of effort for very little payoff. But you're right, the logical place to start is the bedroom and crime scene."

She nodded and went back to work. Her back ached from being hunched over for the past several hours, but she ignored the discomfort, concentrating on finding the proverbial needle in the haystack.

As she worked, her mind drifted to Quinn Murphy. Had he broken the distressing news of Brady's death to the rest of his family? Considering Brady had a different last name than him, she assumed they shared a mother rather than a father. Did Brady have other siblings? Were they huddled close right now, drawing love and support from each other?

She dragged her mind from things that didn't concern her, satisfied when she managed to find a few isolated prints on the rugby trophy, as well as other parts of the room. She did better up in Brady's room, where there was less clutter. Her boss grimaced but helped her collect the beer cans to check for prints. By the time they were finished, they'd probably have more suspects than they'd know what to do with.

Suspects that may or may not lead to the identity of the killer, since there was no guarantee Brady's murderer had left prints at the scene. Still, they didn't have much else to work from. Hair fibers were as much of a nightmare as dusting for prints because of the number of people who'd been in the house, not to mention that Dennis Green's cat shed like crazy in a house that had rarely if ever seen a vacuum.

Running all the fingerprints and hair fibers would take time, so she sent the strips and samples off to the lab for the techs to start working on, prioritizing the ones from the trophy and Brady's room. At the very least, they'd discover if any of the partygoers had criminal records.

Outside, she paused at her car, glancing down at Quinn Murphy's card, debating whether to talk to him now or to go home first to shower and change. She was hungry, having worked the crime scene for almost eight hours straight.

Home first, she decided. Then she'd contact Quinn.

She pulled up to her house, pausing at the mailbox on her way into the driveway. Sometimes she became so lost in her active cases that she forgot to pick up her mail. Today was Sunday, but had she picked it up yesterday? She didn't think so. When she opened the box, she found it was jammed full. As she pulled everything out, a small white envelope with her name printed on the outside, with no postage stamp or return address, made her heart pound heavily in her chest.

Another note. The third in the past two weeks.

She stared at it for a long minute, wishing it was nothing more than a figment of her imagination. But of course it wasn't. She headed inside the house. Even though she was tired and hungry, she used her own kit to dust for prints. She wasn't surprised not to find any.

She hadn't found prints on the previous two notes, either.

Trepidation burned as she opened the envelope flap. Slowly she withdrew the single piece of paper. The message was brief: "I'm coming for you."

Four little words. She dropped the card, struggling to breathe normally as fear clogged her throat. So far, each of the notes she'd received bore a different message.

Guilty as charged.

I'm watching you.

I'm coming for you.

Her knees went weak and she sank into a kitchen chair, struggling not to let fear overwhelm her. Who was doing this? And why? She wanted to think it was some person's strange idea of a joke, but the sinister tone of the notes wasn't easily shrugged off.

Which is exactly what the creep intended. He wanted to scare her. He wanted her to panic. Only a coward would send anonymous notes in the first place. And since she didn't have any men in her life, hadn't so much as had one significant long-term relationship, this had to be connected to her job.

She'd gone through all of her most recent cases, trying to figure out which one may have caused someone to fixate on her. The most likely case was one that had wrapped up two weeks ago, garnering her some media attention. Shanna usually preferred to work behind the scenes, but in this case, the investigation of a well-known cardiac surgeon's murder had cast her reluctantly into the limelight.

The trial had been difficult but her evidence had been solid, and in the end her testimony had caused the jury to find the surgeon's ex-wife, Jessica Markoviack, guilty of murder. But Jessica couldn't be the stalker, since she was currently serving a life sentence in an all-female state prison.

A friend of Jessica's, perhaps? If she remembered right, Jessica had a boyfriend, a guy named Clay Allen who hadn't been involved in the murder, at least according to the evidence. But that didn't mean he wasn't capable of doing the deed. She needed to go back through her case notes, to refresh her memory of the guy's background. He was a viable suspect, someone who had a reason to carry a grudge against her.

Fear gave way to anger as she rose to her feet. Maybe it was time to bring the police into this. The first two notes had been creepy but not outright threatening.

I'm coming for you.

She ground her teeth and turned her back on the note. She'd call the police, even though she knew there was little they could do. Hadn't she already tried to trace the origin of the white cards herself? There was nothing special about them, they were commonly stocked in every office supply store in the area.

Leaving the white card smudged with dark fingerprint powder on the table, she headed down the hall to the bathroom. First she'd shower, and then scrounge around for something to eat. It was only seven-thirty, and she still wanted to interview Quinn.

Focusing her attention on Brady's death would help her to ignore the eerie feeling of someone watching her, no doubt already planning his next move.

Quinn Murphy read through the extensive list of names of all the kids who'd attended Brady's party. The letters blurred and he had to blink to focus.

He rubbed his eyes, forcing himself to stay awake, even though he'd been up for the past thirty-six hours straight. There were already forty-one names on the list, and he was certain there were more that had been forgotten. Kids who'd come only for a few minutes, or those who blended into the woodwork to the point no one ever remembered.

Had the murderer stood back, watching? Waiting for the right moment to strike? He had no way of knowing. Wishing there was at least one solid lead to go on, he picked up the list again. Brady's girlfriend's name was glaringly absent. Anna Belfast had gotten hysterical when he'd told her about Brady's death. No college student, even one in the theater program, could be that good of an actress.

Anna won the lead role of Hannah in *Seven Brides for Seven Brothers* and had done a performance at the theater starting at seven o'clock the night of the party. She'd been irritated that Brady hadn't come to see her and claimed she'd refused to go to his party afterward, choosing to attend a cast get-together after the show instead.

Her alibi was solid, confirmed by several other theater students. Although the suspicious part of his mind insisted there was likely time for her to come to Brady's party after the cast get-together had broken up. Had Anna come to the party to find Brady with another girl? Her roommate, Maggie Carson, also had a role in the play and claimed Anna had come home right afterward, but there was a chance Maggie had lied to cover for Anna. Or Anna could have slipped out even later, after her roommate fell asleep.

Sweet little Anna didn't seem to be the type to bash Brady in the head, but her on-again, off-again relationship with his little brother was enough to keep her on the suspect list.

They didn't have the official report confirming the time of death, but the coroner at the scene had estimated it to be somewhere between five and seven in the morning.

His phone rang, startling him out of his thoughts. He frowned. The number wasn't one he recognized, but he answered it anyway. "Murphy."

"Officer Murphy, this is Shanna Dawson. I'm sorry to call you so late, but the crime scene took much longer than normal to process."

"I'm not surprised." He could easily believe that going through the party mess had taken several long hours. He glanced at his watch and realized it wasn't as late as it felt—just eight-thirty.

"If you're still available, I'd love to talk to you.

But if you'd rather wait until tomorrow, I'd certainly understand."

He pursed his lips, thinking fast. The polite thing to do would be to wait until morning. Shanna had to be as exhausted as he was. But he also knew he wouldn't sleep, couldn't rest until he'd done everything possible to find Brady's killer.

"Tonight is fine." He didn't want to let her off the hook, and there was always the chance she'd give him some details on what they'd found. "Where would you like to meet?"

There was a slight pause before she responded, "I'll meet you at Karly's Kitchen on Dublin Street."

"Sounds good. I can be there in twenty minutes."

"Thanks."

He actually made it in fifteen, but Shanna must live even closer because he found her already seated at a booth, nursing a cup of coffee. He slid in across from her, glancing up as the waitress approached. "I'll have some coffee, too, thanks."

Shanna's face was pale and drawn, as if she'd taken Brady's death as personally as he had. With her wavy dark hair, alabaster skin and wide blue eyes, she reminded him more of a kindergarten teacher than a CSI. Maybe it was the air of innocence clinging to her. He'd thought most law-enforcement types became hardened by the brutal evidence of violence, but Shanna's personality didn't seem to have that distinctive hard edge.

She summoned a smile. "How are you?" she surprised him by asking. "Is your family doing all right?"

Amazed that she cared enough to ask, he sat back in his seat. She couldn't know he wasn't really a part of the family, not in the way she'd meant. His mother had pretty much abandoned him when she'd divorced his father, but over the years he'd made an effort to mend the rift between them, especially once his father died. No matter what, though, he was still an outsider. His mother had found a new life with her second husband, James Wallace, and his half-siblings, Brady and Ivy, were the joys of her life.

And now Brady was dead.

He'd given his mother the news, taking the brunt of her anger and frustration as she railed at him. Knowing that she would have preferred if he was the one who'd died instead of Brady was difficult to ignore.

"I—my mother is taking Brady's death pretty hard, as you can imagine." He tried to soften his gruff tone. He didn't hold a grudge against Brady, even though the kid had been offered every opportunity possible to succeed in life. More than

Quinn had been given, that's for sure. But Brady was basically a good kid.

As Quinn had gotten older, he'd understood how his very presence reminded his mother of her dismal marriage to his father. A fact that was indirectly his fault, since she'd only married his father because she'd gotten pregnant with him.

"I'm sorry for your loss." Shanna surprised him again by reaching across the table to touch the back of his hand in a simple gesture meant to offer comfort. "I'll do everything possible to find Brady's murderer."

"I know." He was impressed by her staunch dedication. And her empathy. Shanna looked young, barely twenty, although he figured with her training and experience she must be at least in her mid-to-late twenties. She was beautiful, her long wavy hair framing a heart-shaped face. The flicker of awareness annoyed him; he was here to help solve Brady's murder, nothing more. "Thanks."

She began the drill, asking about his half brother's life, going over all of Brady's friends and roommates. He gave her everything he knew, which wasn't all that much, since Brady had resented having his older half brother as a campus cop. Brady had kept his distance from Quinn as much as possible. Especially after Quinn had been the one to bust one of Brady's parties a month earlier.

If he'd known about this party last night, he would have busted it, too. And then maybe his brother would still be alive.

Just another reason to feel guilty. Although it wasn't like he was sitting around doing nothing. He'd been investigating a potential sexual assault on a young female student instead.

He pulled his mind to the matter at hand. He told Shanna everything he knew, although it wasn't anything different from what he'd told the detective. Still, working with Shanna as they reviewed the list of kids who'd attended the party made him feel as if he were part of the investigation instead of an innocent bystander.

At ten o'clock, she yawned so wide her jaw popped, and he realized he'd selfishly kept her up long enough. "It's late—we'd better go."

She nodded, signaling the waitress to bring their bill. He knew she intended to pay, but he took the bill from the waitress anyway. "My treat."

Shanna frowned. "You don't have to do that."

"Please, I want to." She couldn't know how much he'd needed to talk to her tonight, to be involved at least this much in the investigation. Besides, he couldn't get into the idea of allowing a woman to pay. Call it old-fashioned, but he didn't care. He stood, waiting for her to precede him out of the diner.

Outside, there were only a few other cars in the postage stamp-size parking lot. His SUV was on the far left end, but she turned toward the right, where a red Toyota Camry was parked next to a row of bushes.

"Thanks, Quinn," she said, formally shaking his hand. "I'll be in touch."

"Sure." Her hand felt small and fragile in his and he released it reluctantly. He followed, intent on making sure she got safely into her car. She only took a few steps though, before suddenly stopping.

She whirled around, coming back toward him. She grabbed his arm in a tight grip. "Do you see him?" she asked in a low, urgent tone. "Do you see the man standing next to my car?"

"Man?" He peered over her shoulder, not seeing any sign of a person, male or otherwise. Had her exhausted mind played tricks on her? "Relax, it's okay. I don't see anyone."

"Are you saying I imagined him?" The sharp edge to her tone made him lift a curious brow.

"No, I believe you. But I don't see him now. Maybe he disappeared behind those bushes."

Abruptly, she let go of his arm, swinging back

to stare at her car. "He's gone. I can't believe I didn't get a better look at him."

Her tone was fierce and brave, but he noticed the slight trembling of her hands. He didn't blame her for being scared; there was no acceptable reason for a man to loiter around a woman's car at ten o'clock at night. Even if she had imagined the guy, he figured she was entitled after such a long day. "I'll walk you to your car."

"I'm fine." She started toward her car with a firm stride, but didn't protest when he caught up to her.

A small white card with her name printed on the outside was stuck beneath the wiper blade on the driver's side. Obviously, her mystery man wasn't her imagination after all.

She gasped in shock and stopped short, staring at the evidence.

"Don't touch anything," he ordered. "We need to call the police, see if we can get some fingerprints off this."

"Don't bother." Her tone was matter of fact.

"What do you mean, don't bother?" What sort of CSI expert was she? "Why not?"

"Because I've gotten several others just like it, and he hasn't left any prints yet."

TWO

Quinn wasn't happy when Shanna insisted on driving home, but he followed right behind her as they went the couple of blocks to her house. She lived in a nice, if older, suburb of Chicago, where the houses were small and the lots even smaller, yet well-groomed. He gripped the steering wheel tightly, anxious to get to the bottom of this.

The brief glimpse of fear in Shanna's eyes tugged at him. He'd seen the same haunted expression in the young freshman's eyes last night, after the attack. His stomach squeezed. He didn't like the possibility of Shanna suffering a similar experience. Thankfully, the mystery man had only left a note and hadn't touched her.

Some people felt that campus police officers weren't the real deal, hiding from the true crime that stalked the city streets. He'd done his stint as a city cop for over six years. Now he preferred to proactively protect the younger, innocent college kids rather than taking criminals off the street, knowing there was always another cop eager to take his place.

He pulled into Shanna's driveway right behind her, and hurried out of his car to stop her from going inside. "Stay back. I want to check things out first."

She pushed his hand away. "I'm a trained law-enforcement officer," she protested.

"Yeah, but I'm armed." And he'd noticed she wasn't, at least not at the restaurant. She had carried a gun while she was investigating the crime scene as all CSIs were required to do. But knowing she was a trained officer didn't matter. For some reason, this woman raised his protective instincts to full alert.

She stared at him for a long minute and then took a step back, allowing him to take the lead. While she hovered behind him, he took the key from her fingers and ventured inside. The layout was a simple ranch design; the side door entered into the kitchen. The front door opened into the living room, and then there was a short hallway leading to the bedrooms.

The light over the kitchen sink was burning bright so he swept his gaze over the room, listening intently. His gut told him the place was empty, but he went through each room anyway, just to make sure.

When he finished, he headed back to the kitchen. Three notes were sitting in the center of the table. He leaned over, read them and then looked up at her askance. "Have you called the police about these threats?"

She winced and shook her head, her arms wrapped around her torso as if she were cold. "Not yet. I was going to, though. That last one came today. I mean, yesterday." She frowned. "Actually, I don't exactly know what day it came, because I sometimes forget to pick up the mail."

"So you received a note and still drove out to meet me tonight?" His fingers curled into helpless fists at her foolishness. "Are you crazy?"

Her shrug was nonchalant. "Working on Brady's case helped keep my mind off my problems."

A stalker wasn't just any old problem. He was tempted to snap at her, but realized Shanna was a trained law-enforcement agent, just like he was. She could take care of herself.

So why did he want to do that for her?

Because he was tempted to pull her into the shelter of his arms in a gesture of comfort, he forced himself to stay where he was, keeping a safe distance between them.

"Do you have any idea who's sending these?"

he asked in a low tone. "A jilted boyfriend? Someone at work that you refused to go out with?"

She made a strangled sound. "No. I haven't been seeing anyone, no ex-boyfriends. No one's been bothering me. My personal life is dull and uneventful. To be honest, I've already concluded the notes have to be related to one of my cases."

He shouldn't have been relieved to know there wasn't a man in her life, just as he shouldn't have noticed how vulnerable she'd looked when she'd admitted the boring details of her past. Why was such a pretty woman leading a dull and uneventful life? Her personal life was none of his business, but he wanted to know just the same. He kept his voice firm. "You need to call the police."

"You're the police," she joked weakly.

"Shanna." He moved closer, lifting his hand to brush her hair away from her cheek. "You know I don't have jurisdiction here. You need to call this in, before this guy gets too close."

For a moment she simply stared at him with something forlorn in her gaze, but then she pulled back and straightened her shoulders. "Don't worry. I won't let him get to me."

He wanted to believe her. But that hint of vulnerability made him hesitate. Maybe because he was a pushover for a woman in distress. Yet she seemed just as determined to stand alone. A part of him admired her independence while another part of him was annoyed at her stubborn foolishness.

"Are you going to call the police?" he asked for the third time.

"Not right now. It's late. I'll wait until the morning. This isn't an emergency and there isn't anything they're going to be able to do about the notes tonight. Especially since I can't even give them a reasonable description of the suspect."

He knew she was right, but that didn't make it any easier for him to leave. He glanced around her small living room. "I don't like leaving you here alone."

"I'll be fine." The underlying steel in her tone finally convinced him.

"Okay, but do me a favor." He held her gaze, imploring her to listen to reason. "Close and lock every window."

She grimaced and nodded. "I like having the cool fresh air from outside coming through the windows, but I'll manage without for tonight," she reluctantly agreed.

He waited until she'd gone through every room, closing and locking the windows. Standing in the kitchen, his gaze continued to linger on the notes.

Who could have sent them? And why? Someone who liked to play games, obviously. Mind games. The thought caused a sick feeling to settle in his gut.

"All set?" he asked when she came back toward him.

"Yes. Thanks for following me home."

"You're welcome." He forced himself to walk toward the side door. "You have my cell-phone number. Promise you'll call if you need anything."

She smiled. "Don't worry. I'll be fine."

He told himself she was right. She would be fine. Outside he paused and listened, satisfied to hear the dead bolt click into place. He headed toward his car, glancing back to look at her house. She'd shut off most of the lights, except maybe the one in her bedroom, which he couldn't see from the street.

He slid behind the wheel and backed out of her driveway, intent on going home when he saw a car moving slowly down the street. Too slowly. Heart thudding in his chest, he pulled over to the side of the road, holding his breath as he waited. The car passed him by, turning into a driveway several houses down. The garage door opened, and the car disappeared inside.

"Idiot," he muttered to himself. He was exhausted, had been up for over forty hours straight, but he couldn't just go home.

Shutting off the car, he pulled the key out of

the ignition and leaned his seat as far back as it could go. He cracked the windows so he could hear better, knowing he was going to spend the night here, watching over Shanna, despite her refusal to accept his help.

He was too tired to drive anyway.

Slouched in his car, he stared at Shanna's dark house, wondering about her. Why was she so alone when she lived in a nice neighborhood that seemed like the perfect place to raise a family? The pain shadowing her eyes hadn't all been from the notes, he was certain. Yet as much as he wanted to protect her, she seemed just as determined to brush off his help.

Rubbing his eyes, he briefly wished for peace rather than being haunted by the demons in his past. His dad had been a city cop for years. Hunting drug runners, witnessing armed robberies and murders, had taken its toll. His dad had turned to booze, ignoring the abuse he'd inflicted on his body until one day Quinn had come home to find his dad crumpled on the bathroom floor, lying in a pool of blood.

He'd called 911 but had already known it was too late. According to the coroner, his dad had been throwing up blood from some burst blood vessel in his esophagus, and had literally choked on it before he'd died.

The memory haunted him ever since.

Quinn had always avoided alcohol, but then he went a step further, giving up the stress of being a city cop to join the university campus police force. His mother had wanted him to get out of law enforcement altogether, claiming his dad's job had ruined their marriage, but he couldn't do it.

There was a part of him that needed to know he made a difference in the world, no matter how small and insignificant it may be.

His attraction to Shanna, though, forced him to remember all the reasons he veered away from relationships. He wasn't a safe bet, and not just because of his family history of alcoholism. He knew from firsthand experience that women wanted a man who came home every night. Men who weren't in danger. Men who didn't obsess over their work. Even as a campus cop, he'd been drawn on by gang members with guns more times than he could count. Most recently by two idiots who decided to rob the corner coffee shop.

Leslie had left him, just like his mother had left his father. Proving he was better off alone.

With a sigh, he let his head fall back against the seat rest, unable to prevent himself from closing his eyes. He'd stay here outside Shanna's place, making sure she called the police to report her stalker first thing in the morning. Once he was satisfied she'd taken steps to assure her safety, he'd go back to working Brady's murder investigation where he'd left off.

Finding out who'd killed Brady had to remain his top priority.

Shanna didn't sleep very well; the slightest noises kept waking her up. All because she'd let the creepy stalker get to her more than she'd wanted to admit.

At least she'd held it together in front of Quinn. He was too attractive for her peace of mind. Not handsome per se, but definitely ruggedly attractive. On top of that, he'd been nice, supportive. Not that she needed his help.

What she needed was action. Today she'd get a full investigation going on this note-writing guy, whoever he was. Stalking was against the law, as were threats. She'd find this guy and hand him over to the police the first chance she had.

With renewed determination, she took a quick shower and spent a few minutes blow-drying her hair before heading to the kitchen, intending to brew a pot of coffee.

As she walked past the entryway to the living room, she happened to glance through the large picture window overlooking the street. She froze, her heart leaping into her throat when she noticed the SUV parked directly across the street from her house. The car stood out because her neighbors across the street were elderly and didn't drive. Fearing the worst, she grabbed her cell phone and almost punched the numbers for 911 when she realized why the car looked familiar.

It was the same car that had followed her home last night. The vehicle belonged to Quinn. Flipping her cell phone shut, she crossed over to the picture window in time to see Quinn yawning and stretching his arms over his head. While she was staring at him, he glanced toward her house, capturing her gaze. For a moment, the strange connection between them seemed to shimmer in the air.

Had he really slept out there all night? She was touched by his chivalry but was determined not to read more into his actions than the situation warranted. Uncertainly, she opened the front door. Was she supposed to invite him in after the way he'd slept in his car to protect her?

He climbed awkwardly from the car, his limbs obviously stiff from the cramped seat. But then he came straight toward her, meeting her halfway. "Morning, Shanna. Did you sleep well?"

She tried to act nonchalant. "Better than you, I'd be willing to bet. Quinn, it was very sweet of you to sleep in your car, but I told you I'd be fine."

"I know, but I was too tired to drive," he said, glancing longingly over her shoulder. "Is that coffee I smell?"

"Yes." She felt bad about the exhaustion shadowing his features. As uncomfortable as she was having him there, the least she could do was feed him. "Come on in, there's plenty to share."

He followed her inside, crossing the living room to the kitchen. He took a seat at her table, and she could feel his gaze on her as she filled a mug from the coffeemaker. She couldn't help feeling self-conscious with him there, maybe because she'd never had a man in her house. Ever.

She carefully set the mug on the table, thankful she didn't spill. "Ah, do you like eggs? Because I have to tell you, there isn't a huge variety of food to choose from."

"Eggs would be great." His stomach rumbled loudly, as if reinforcing his need for food. He flashed a sheepish grin and her heart did a funny little flip.

She squelched the reaction and quickly threw together scrambled eggs and toast. The sooner she gave him food, the sooner she could send him on his way.

When he'd finished the first cup of coffee, he came over to get a refill. His closeness was enough to rattle her, and she burned her thumb on the edge of the frying pan. She swallowed a yelp, thrusting her thumb under a stream of cold water. This was ridiculous; there was no reason to be nervous.

"Are you all right?" he asked.

"Fine." She forced a smile. "The eggs are just about ready."

"Thanks." He carried his mug over to the table, and she handed him a plate full of eggs and toast. They ate in silence for a few minutes before Quinn spoke up. "You're going to call the police when we're finished with breakfast, right?"

She barely refrained from rolling her eyes. The man sounded like a broken record. "Right."

As soon as she finished her meal, Shanna gave in and pulled out her cell phone. Considering she'd worked all day Sunday, she could afford to be a little late to work this morning. She had to look up the nonemergency number in the phone book and briefly explained her situation when one of the officers came on the line.

"They're sending someone over," she said, hanging up a few minutes later. "They asked me to leave the card from last night under the windshield wiper." She hadn't touched the note, figuring the cops would want to see exactly where the guy had left it.

"Good." Quinn sat back, sipping his coffee as if he wasn't in a hurry to leave.

"The police are on their way, Quinn. There's no need for you to stay." She carried her dirty dishes to the sink, cleaning up the remains of their breakfast mess. "You need to go home, get some decent sleep."

"How long before you get anything back from the lab?" he asked, ignoring her blatant hint urging him to go. "On the fingerprints and hair fibers?"

"We have lots of evidence to sift through. I'm afraid it will probably be awhile." She understood how anxious he was for news, any news. She'd been on his side of the waiting game. It had only been in recent years that she'd learned how patience was a virtue. "I promise I'll get in touch with you if we come up with anything."

He glanced at her. "You know I'm not really involved in this investigation, except peripherally. All of your evidence needs to go to Hank Nelson."

"I know." She wrung out the dishrag and turned toward him, resting her hip against the counter. "But you're the one who knows the students on campus, right? Hank has to keep you involved in the investigation to a certain extent. Maybe we do have to give all the evidence to the lead homicide detective on the case, but I see no reason why the crime lab wouldn't cooperate with the campus police, too."

He smiled and shrugged. "Hank probably won't like it, but I'll take anything you can give me."

His appreciation warmed her heart. After the way he'd slept in his car, just to protect her, this was the least she could do in return. Besides, the homicide had taken place on his turf. She'd expect the same consideration in his shoes.

Their gazes locked, and for a moment she felt as if she couldn't breathe. She didn't deserve to feel this attraction to him, but she couldn't look away. If she were honest, she'd admit she intended to keep him in the loop because she wanted to see him again, not just because of professional courtesy.

The ringing of her doorbell echoed through the house, breaking the moment. She swallowed hard and pushed away from the counter, crossing over to the living room to open the front door.

The officers who stood there had their respective IDs ready, which she carefully inspected before allowing Officers Kappas and Jones inside.

"Murphy?" Jones, the taller of the two, frowned when he recognized Quinn. "Haven't seen you since your old man's funeral." His gaze landed on Shanna, frankly curious. "I—uh—didn't know you were involved with anyone."

Funeral? Shanna glanced at Quinn in surprise, but then flushed when she realized the two officers assumed she and Quinn were a couple. "He's a friend," she said quickly.

The last thing she needed were rumors going around about her and Quinn. How embarrassing *that* would be.

"We were at Karly's Kitchen last night when Ms. Dawson saw a man loitering by her car," Quinn said, as if sensing her discomfort. "I didn't see him, but we found a white envelope with her name printed on the front in block letters, stuck under her windshield."

She was grateful Quinn cut to the chase, putting the interview back on track.

"Ms. Dawson has received other notes, as well." He picked up the three notes she'd left on the counter and handed them to the officers. "Shanna, when did you get the first note?"

"Two weeks ago." She explained how the first note had actually showed up in her mailbox down at the CSI lab. The message read "Guilty as charged," so she hadn't really thought too much about it. "I guess I figured the sender was just someone dealing with a lot of anger. The second and third ones, though, were in my mailbox here at home."

Her personal space. Her haven.

"You dusted for fingerprints?" Kappas asked.

"I'm a CSI—of course I dusted for prints. Didn't find any, though. I also tried to narrow down the source of the paper, but it's carried everywhere." She lifted her palms helplessly. "Really, this could be related to any one of my cases, although the one I just wrapped up, the Markoviack murder, is the most likely one."

"Did the man by your car look at all familiar?" Jones took over the questioning.

"I only caught a glimpse, but didn't recognize him at all."

"You mentioned this being related to one of your cases, like the Markoviack murder. Why does that one stand out in your mind?" Kappas asked.

She quickly explained about the last big case she'd worked on, how her evidence put Jessica Markoviack in prison. Both officers exchanged a look and agreed that Jessica's former boyfriend was a possible culprit.

"Where's the fourth note now?" Jones asked.

She glanced at Quinn. "We left it beneath the windshield wiper. My car is in the garage." Leading the way out the side door, to the detached garage where her Toyota Camry was parked, she gestured to the car.

The officers looked at the note, then used gloved hands to remove it from beneath the wiper blade. She took out her fingerprint kit and dusted both the note and the windshield for prints.

There weren't any, just like the previous notes.

Jones opened the flap and removed the note. They crowded around to see what it said. "Next time, you'll be alone," Jones read out loud.

"I don't get it," Quinn muttered. "How did he know you were with me?"

She couldn't suppress a shiver, fear congealing in the bottom of her stomach. "Because he's watching me."

Kappas and Jones exchanged a grim look. "I'll recommend increased surveillance of this neighborhood, ma'am," Jones said.

Sending a patrol car through every couple hours wasn't going to prevent this guy from trying to get her, but she understood they were doing the best they could. "That's fine."

"No, it's not," Quinn argued bluntly. "If this guy is watching you, he'll know to hide from the police. You need a bodyguard. Or at least a comprehensive security system."

"Maybe." She didn't want to admit his idea had merit. "I'll think about it."

Quinn looked as if he wanted to argue, but instead he turned toward the officers. "Anything else?"

"Ms. Dawson might want to find a friend to

stay with for a while," Officer Jones said. "Being here alone is asking for trouble."

Friends? She almost laughed. The only real friend she had was Megan O'Ryan, and she'd recently moved to Crystal Lake, Wisconsin. Megan had just gotten married, and after everything her friend had been through, Shanna couldn't bring herself to dump her own troubles on Megan's shoulders. Megan had barely survived being strangled by a serial killer. Worse, the killer was someone they knew. Raoul Lee was a brilliant scientist. Now he'd spend the rest of his life in jail. The cops waited expectantly, so she nodded. "I'll see what I can do."

The officers left, promising to be in touch if they found anything.

"I'll follow you to work." Quinn's tone didn't leave room for discussion.

His persistence was starting to annoy her. But rather than arguing, she gathered her work stuff together, including her shoulder holster. She sensed Quinn's frustration as he stood watching her. Before she could get out the door, her cell phone rang.

She recognized Alan's number from the lab. Setting her laptop case on the kitchen table, she answered the phone. "Do you have something for me, Al?"

"Yeah, uh, we got a hit on one of the finger-prints found at your college frat house crime scene."

A hit on the fingerprints was good news. "Who is it?" she asked eagerly, glancing at Quinn. An identity would get them one step closer to find-ing the killer.

"Are you on your way here? Because I think we should talk in person." He cleared his throat loudly. "The news is going to be a bit of a shock."

His tap-dancing around the issue only irritated her. "Just tell me."

There was a pause. "Shanna, we have a set of fingerprints matching a child who's been missing for fourteen years."

A child? Missing for fourteen years? No. Oh, no. Her stomach twisted, and little red dots swam in her vision. She grabbed the edge of the kitchen table and pushed the word through her tight throat. "Who?"

"Your sister. Skylar Dawson."

THREE

Shanna blinked, staring up at Quinn's anxious face looming over her. The kitchen floor was hard and unyielding beneath her back. Disoriented, she winced and lifted her head. "What happened?"

"You fainted." Quinn's gruff tone betrayed his concern.

"Fainted?" Embarrassed, she pushed up onto her elbows, her head throbbing. She must have hit her head on the floor.

"Let me help you up." Quinn put his arm around her shoulders, supporting her weight as she struggled to her feet. Her knees still felt wobbly, so she sat at the kitchen table.

"What happened?" Quinn asked, picking up her cell phone from where it must have skittered across the floor. "One minute you were saying something about the fingerprint results from the crime scene, and the next you collapsed onto the floor."

In a rush it all came flooding back.

Skylar. The pressure in her chest built to the point she could barely breathe. Her fault. It was her fault her little sister had been kidnapped fourteen years ago. Her fault that her parents had divorced, destroying what was left of their family.

"Shanna, breathe," Quinn commanded in a sharp tone.

Feeling dizzy again, she obeyed, taking a deep breath before she did something stupid, like fainting for a second time. After a few minutes the room stopped spinning.

Forcing herself to meet his questioning gaze, she knew she couldn't lie to him. Not now. Not about this. "The prints at the scene of Brady's death match those of my sister, Skylar."

Quinn frowned, perplexed. "Okay. Does your sister go to Carlyle University, too?"

"I don't know." She licked her dry lips. "Skylar was kidnapped when she was only five years old. Her case has remained unsolved. I haven't seen her in fourteen years. No one has."

Quinn's jaw dropped, and he sank into the chair beside her. "You're kidding."

"No. I'm not." The memory burned with a clarity that belied the passing years.

On Skylar's first day of kindergarten, her mother had insisted Shanna take her sister all the way inside the elementary school to meet the kindergarten teacher. She was older by five years, so Shanna had agreed. As they'd approached the school, she'd discovered a bunch of her friends were playing kickball on the older kid's section of the playground, farthest from the building.

"Shanna!" Toby Meyers, the boy she secretly liked, had waved and shouted to her from the game. "Hurry up, we're losing. We need you on our team."

Thrilled that he'd noticed her, and that he'd wanted her on his team, she'd dropped Skylar's hand. "Just go inside the building there, Skylar, okay? You'll see Mrs. Anderson, the kindergarten teacher, in the first classroom."

"But Shanna," Skylar protested, hanging back.

"Just go!" Impatiently, Shanna had given Skylar a little push and then turned away, rushing over to join the kickball game already in progress. Toby made room for her in the lineup to kick next.

She'd taken her turn, kicking the ball with all her strength, sending it sailing over the heads of all the kids. With Toby cheering her on, she'd rounded the bases, making it all the way home to score.

They hadn't won the game—the bell had rung and they'd had to quit—but Toby's cheering had echoed in her head for the next hour. Until the school principal, Mrs. Haggerty, had tapped her on the shoulder, taking her out of her fourth-grade class to the office.

"Shanna, when did you last see your sister?"

Skylar? Guiltily, Shanna realized she hadn't even thought about her sister since hurrying off to the kickball game. "This morning, when I walked her to school."

"Did you take her inside to see the teacher?"

Numbly, Shanna shook her head no.

"She's not in the kindergarten class." Mrs. Haggerty looked extremely worried. "Your mother is on her way here. I think we'd better search every classroom. Maybe Skylar got lost and is hiding somewhere."

Shanna felt sick, knowing her mother would be so angry that she hadn't taken Skylar all the way inside the classroom as she'd been told to do. Mrs. Haggarty had hurried away to begin searching for her sister, but she'd just sat in the principal's office, afraid to do anything, hoping and praying they'd find Skylar hiding as they thought.

But her little sister hadn't been hiding. Nobody had seen Skylar anywhere around the school. Shanna had been the last person to see her sister alive and well.

Now she was gone. And it was all her fault.

"Here, drink this." Quinn thrust a glass in her hands.

Blinking at him, she willed the guilt-laden memories away. She took the glass and drank, reveling in the cool water soothing her throat. "Thanks. I'm fine."

"No!" Quinn's tone was sharp. "You're not fine. You're pale, as if you're going to faint again."

"I won't," she protested. She refused to faint again; once was certainly bad enough. She needed to pull herself together. The reality of the situation finally sank into her brain. Her sister's prints were found at the scene. After fourteen years of not knowing anything, those fingerprints meant that Skylar was alive. Alive!

Closing her eyes, she bowed her head and probed the depths of her soul, dragging out the faith she shouldn't have given up on, praying for the first time in years. *Lord, thank You for showing me that Skylar is alive. And please guide me. Give me the strength and courage to find my sister.*

"Shanna?" Quinn's tone was anxious.

She lifted her head and forced a smile. "It's a gift, Quinn. A true gift. After all this time, we finally found Skylar. I have to call my mother, to let her know the news." And her father. He'd flat-out refused to talk to her when she'd tried to get in touch with him a few weeks ago, but surely he'd talk to her now.

"Whoa, wait a minute." Quinn took her hand in his, halting her from surging to her feet. "Why don't we wait until we know what we're dealing with?"

"Are you kidding?" Shanna stared at him, tugging at her hand. "My sister is *alive.* Do you know how many years we've waited to know even that much?" She was ashamed to admit she'd thought the worst. That Skylar was lying dead and buried in an abandoned field somewhere. At any moment she'd expected the police to uncover her bones.

God, forgive me for losing faith. Forgive me for believing Skylar was dead.

"Yes, she's alive. But we don't know where she's been for all these years. And I highly doubt she's going by the name of Skylar Dawson. Besides, her fingerprints were found at a crime scene, which makes her one of the many suspects in Brady's death."

Skylar a suspect? No, it wasn't possible. But Shanna slid back into her seat, the sick feeling in her stomach persisting. No. There was no way she believed her long-lost sister was a murderer. "Skylar didn't hurt your brother."

Quinn's glance held a trace of sympathy. "Maybe not, but take a moment to think this through. What can you really tell your mother at this point? You don't know what name Skylar is using these days. We don't even have a photo yet. Why don't we go through the names of the kids who were known to be at the party? We can get their ID pictures from the school, and you can see if any of the girls look familiar."

She had to admit, his idea had merit. And she had enough vacation time to get out of doing the routine lab work. Besides, now that her sister's prints had been found, Eric would remove her from actively working the case.

"Maybe we can even get a younger picture of your sister to perform a computer aging process," Quinn continued. "Once you know Skylar's current name, you'll have really good news to tell your mother."

She bit her lip and nodded, knowing he was right to take things slow. But she wanted to find Skylar now. Her patience was nonexistent after fourteen years. "My mother has a computer age-progression image of Skylar—it's posted on the website for missing children. But first I still need to go to the lab. I need to find out exactly where Skylar's prints were found."

"I'll go with you." Quinn released her hand and rose to his feet.

She stood, taking her phone from his hand. Skylar's prints were found at a college house. How ironic to know Skylar was here at a local university, only twenty miles from home after all these years.

Did Skylar remember her? Or their parents?

She almost hoped not, because that would mean Skylar had suffered, missing her home and her family while being taken somewhere else.

Her stomach clenched as the worst-case scenario flashed through her head. She dearly hoped that Skylar's life since she'd been gone had been decent and good.

Not dark and twisted.

Quinn kept a wary eye on Shanna as he drove to the CSI crime lab. Her face was still pale, but she looked a little less fragile than she had lying cold on the floor of her kitchen. She'd taken years off his life when she'd fainted like that. Although, after hearing her long-lost sister's fingerprints were found at Brady's crime scene, he certainly understood why she'd reacted the way she did.

He couldn't imagine how awful it must have been to lose a younger sibling to a kidnapping, never knowing if she was alive or dead.

Dead. Like Brady. His fingers tightened on the steering wheel. Quinn knew he should be heading over to his mother's offering his support, rather than sticking close to Shanna's side, but he couldn't in good conscience leave her alone. Besides, staying with Shanna meant he might get more information related to Brady's case, which was what he wanted.

Satisfied with his decision, he turned his head from side to side, trying to ease the kinks from his neck. He wasn't interested in Shanna's mysterious past unless it had a direct bearing on Brady's murder. Although for the life of him, he couldn't see anything but a random connection. But if Skylar disappeared fourteen years ago, she would be nineteen now. Just a year younger than Brady. Interesting.

Pulling up in front of the state crime-lab building, Quinn glanced at her. "Is it okay if I come in with you?"

"Sure." She glanced at him in surprise. "We'll register you for a visitor pass."

Intrigued by what they might find out inside the crime lab, he followed Shanna as she headed to her buddy Al, the fingerprint analyst.

"Shanna?" A tall, thin middle-aged man hurried over. "I've been waiting for you. I ran these prints first thing this morning. Come here— you have to look at this fingerprint comparison for yourself."

"I believe you," she protested, going along with him anyway. She peered at the computer screen for a long moment as if afraid to believe the truth. "You're convinced there's no way this could be a mistake?"

"None." Al went on to explain exactly which pattern in the fingerprint made them unique. "Despite the size difference between an adult and a child, they're definitely the same."

"What part of the crime scene did this print come from?" Shanna asked.

Al's glance slid from hers and he grimaced. "Now, don't be upset, but I found her fingerprints on both the rugby trophy and the desk in the victim's room."

She sucked in a harsh breath. Quinn crossed over to stand beside her, since it seemed she'd forgotten his presence. "Don't jump to conclusions," he warned. "There might be a legitimate reason for her prints to be on the trophy."

"True enough," Al chimed in. "We found a total of four prints on the trophy, one from the victim, one from your sister and two others. After we get all the kids identified, we'll start getting copies of their prints in the system, to see what matches."

Shanna nodded, although Quinn could tell she was badly shaken by the news. She asked,

"Do you have anything else to go on? Any other fingerprint matches?"

"Not yet," Al admitted. "I started with the trophy and the kid's bedroom, and so far, your sister is the only match I've gotten from the database, aside from the victim's, of course. Getting through the rest of the house is going to take some time."

"I understand." Shanna fell silent.

Al looked at her with sympathy. "I already informed Eric about this. He told you to take off as much time as you need."

Shanna nodded as if she were still in a daze.

"Do you need to do anything else?" Quinn asked, putting a hand on her arm. "Or do we have time to head over to the admissions office of Carlyle University to look at photo IDs?"

"The admissions office," she agreed. "Al? If you find anything else, please let me know."

"I will." The older scientist gazed at her with true concern. "If you need to talk, I'm here."

A slight smile flitted around her mouth. "Thanks. Let Eric know I'll be in touch later."

Clearly, Shanna was close to Al, and he found himself wondering about her family as they walked back outside to his SUV. She'd mentioned her mother, but not her father. "This news is really going to shock your family, isn't it?"

"Yes," she murmured, sliding into the passenger seat as he climbed in behind the wheel. "My mother always clung to the belief Skylar was alive, but my dad refused to even talk about her. My parents divorced a few years after Skylar's kidnapping, mostly because of my dad."

His heart squeezed in sympathy. "I know what it's like to come from a broken home."

"Maybe, but at least you know the breakup wasn't your fault." The faint bitterness in her tone surprised him.

Her fault? He shot her a quick glance. "Shanna, I'm sure your parents didn't blame you."

Her gaze was bleak. "Yes, they did. Because it was true. Skylar's kidnapping was my fault." She turned away, staring out the window. "You were right to hold off on telling my mother. I want to find my sister first. I can't bear to raise her hopes for no reason."

He reached over to take her hand in his. "Maybe looking through the student IDs will help."

"I hope so," she murmured. "I need to be able to give my mother that much."

He didn't know what to say to that. His cell phone rang, and he juggled the steering wheel, going against state law by answering it. "Hello?"

"Quinn?" His mother's shrill voice echoed in his ear. "Where are you?"

"I'm following up on some leads from Brady's case," he told her, trying to ignore that she hadn't bothered asking how he was doing. His mother tended to live in a world that was centered on herself and her second family. Not the mistake of her first marriage. "What's wrong? Are you and James doing all right?"

"It's been awful to sit here not knowing anything. We've been waiting for you to bring us some news." Her tone was full of reproach.

"I wish I had some news to bring you, but I don't." He maneuvered the car around a turn with one hand, refraining from reminding her that Brady had been dead for just a little more than twenty-four hours. "Look, Mom, I have to go. I'm driving. After I go through the list of kids who were at Brady's party, I'll be in touch."

"Call us the minute you find anything. We have an appointment at the funeral home this evening, but we don't know when they're going to release Brady's body." Her tone grew thick with suppressed tears.

Guilt swirled as he realized he should be making the funeral arrangements for her. "I'll help you with the arrangements, Mom. I'll find out when they're going to release Brady's body, and I'll meet you at the funeral home when I finish here."

"All right. I'll let James know the plan." His mother hung up. Fighting a surge of helplessness that he couldn't do more, Quinn flipped his phone shut.

"I can look through the photo IDs myself," Shanna offered in a low tone. "Sounds as if you have a lot to do at home."

Selfishly, he didn't want to leave Shanna. Not yet. Not until he knew whether or not she'd recognized any of the photo IDs as potentially belonging to her sister.

"I have time. Let's go through the pictures first, see if anyone looks even vaguely familiar. For now we'll use whatever aged photo your mom has posted on the missing children website."

"Sounds good."

Quinn parked in a no-parking zone, using his campus police tag to identify his car, and walked inside the main registration office with Shanna at his side. It was busy for a Monday, but within moments they were granted access to the library and the database where the computer records of all the college students' information and photos were kept.

"Here's the list of partygoers," Quinn said, pushing the list in front of her. At least half the attendees were female. "Let's start with these first."

She nodded, and he typed in the first name on

the computer. After a few seconds, the photograph popped up on the screen. Shanna stared at the image so long, he cast a concerned glance her way. "What's wrong?"

"Nothing." Shanna slowly shook her head. "It's just that other than Skylar's brown eyes, I don't even know what to look for. Her hair could be any length, any color."

"Brown eyes?" He raised a brow, peering at her. No contacts that he could see. "Yours are blue."

"Yeah. Skylar takes after my dad. He has brown eyes. Mine and my mom's are blue."

"I see. We could narrow the search function to just those girls with brown eyes."

"No." She put her hand on his arm, stopping him. "I'd like to see them all, if you don't mind."

He hesitated, but then nodded. His time constraints weren't hers. After all these years, Shanna deserved at least a couple of hours to get through the list. "Okay."

One by one, she paged through the list of girls who'd been identified as attending the party. A few times she toggled back and forth between the picture of how Skylar might look now and the actual student photo, but in the end she sat back, slowly shaking her head.

"None of them look familiar." Her dejected tone

made him empathize with what she must be going through. "I thought…" She didn't finish.

"Hey, we've only gone through the party list. There are thousands of other female student pictures to get through." He didn't have time to get through the rest now, but he could come back later, after the visit to the funeral home.

"Maybe." Shanna lifted her tortured gaze. "Looking at these pictures is harder than I thought. I should recognize her. My own sister. The image should jump out at me, don't you think?"

"Try to relax," he soothed. "We still have time—"

"No! You don't understand! It's already been fourteen years. I have to find her, Quinn. I have to!"

FOUR

Shanna stared at Quinn, feeling the pressure building up in her chest, preventing her from breathing. At the same time, her pulse skyrocketed into triple digits. For a moment she was helpless, unable to fight the overwhelming sense of panic.

Fourteen years! She'd waited fourteen years to hear news about her sister, and she was so close. Her sister was here, somewhere on this college campus. She couldn't fail to recognize her now. *She couldn't.*

"Easy, Shanna, breathe," Quinn said in his low, hypnotic voice. "This isn't the time to have a panic attack."

Panic attack? What was he talking about? "I'm not!" she snapped. The flash of anger at Quinn helped loosen the tightness in her chest. But her breathing was still shaky.

His green-gold gaze held a note of sympathy.

"It's okay. You've certainly been through a lot over the past few hours."

She closed her eyes, feeling like the worst kind of basket case, and concentrated on breathing. Deep breath in, hold for ten seconds before exhaling slowly. She repeated the process several times, calming herself and realizing Quinn was right. She was having a panic attack.

Earlier today, she'd fainted for the first time ever, and now this. What in the world was wrong with her? She needed to pull herself together, or she wouldn't be any good to Skylar. She needed to remember she was a trained crime-scene investigator.

Not a victim. Not anymore. Her sister was alive. And she'd need every one of her investigative skills to find her.

"I'm fine," she murmured when he lightly rested his hand on her shoulder in apparent concern. She opened her eyes and lifted her head to glance up at him sheepishly. "I'm sorry. I'm not usually this much of a mess."

"Shanna, cut yourself some slack already, would you?" Quinn stared at her with mild exasperation. "First you have some creepy guy following you, and then you discover your long-lost sister is alive. I think you're entitled to lose control a bit."

For the first time in what seemed like hours, she cracked a small smile. "Thanks, Quinn. But that's not a good excuse. I'm not the type to fall apart like this."

He scowled in disagreement. "If that's not a good excuse, I don't know what is."

Slowly she shook her head. Suddenly, everything fell into place, crystal clear. "No, this is God's way of reminding me I can't succeed on my own. For years I didn't put all my heart, soul and faith in God, and now I realize how wrong that was. It's about time I face the truth. I need to put my fears and my worries into God's hands. With His support and guidance we'll find Skylar." Even as she said the words, Shanna felt calmer. More at peace.

How could she have forgotten the power of prayer? How could she have abandoned her faith when she needed it the most? No wonder she'd started falling apart.

Quinn's eyes widened as if he were surprised by what she'd said, and then he physically pulled away and averted his gaze. "So, how about I drive you home?" He glanced up at the clock on the wall. "I need to leave now to meet my mother and her husband at the funeral home."

His withdrawal and the abrupt way he'd changed the subject was a response she hadn't anticipated.

Clearly, Quinn wasn't comfortable talking about faith and God. Because he didn't believe in God? Or the power of prayer? While she could relate to a certain extent, hadn't she made a similar mistake over these past few years? She still found it unbearably sad that Quinn might not believe in God at all.

But she wasn't brave enough to broach the subject now. Not when he clearly had other problems crowding his mind. Like planning his brother's funeral.

"No thanks. I'm going to stay for a while," she said lightly, turning back toward the computer screen. "I want to make a dent in these photos."

"There's plenty of time for that tomorrow," he started, but she cut him off.

"No. I'm staying." She wasn't the weak woman who'd suffered from a panic attack just a few minutes ago. Already she felt stronger, more determined. With God's help and support she could do anything. She forced a reassuring smile. "Don't worry about me. I'll catch a cab home when I'm finished here."

He stared at her for several tense moments before letting out a heavy sigh. "I'd rather you wait for me," he protested. "How about if I come back here to pick you up after we're finished with the funeral arrangements?"

"I'm fine with taking a cab, Quinn. You don't need to go out of your way."

He scowled with frustration. "Wait for me," he repeated with more force this time. "I'll pick you up when you're finished here, okay?"

With only a slight shrug in response, she kept her gaze glued to the computer screen as she started with the female students at the beginning of the alphabet. Abbot, Carrie? Not a match. Abel, Rebecca? Not a match.

She knew exactly when Quinn left, the library door shutting quietly behind him.

Glancing back, she watched him through the glass door, fighting the urge to call him back. There was no need to keep dragging him into her problems. He should be with his family right now.

It would be in her best interest to remember that finding Skylar was her priority, not his.

Quinn drove west to the Life-Everlasting Chapel, the place his mother had chosen to handle Brady's funeral arrangements.

As he drove, Shanna's words about trusting God tumbled through his mind. For some odd reason, he was surprised to hear about her faith in God.

He hadn't been inside a church in years, since before his parents' marriage had crumbled. A happy memory from long ago crept into his mind. He'd been about four or five years old and had attended church with his parents. Afterward, they'd gone out for breakfast, and he remembered walking between them, holding each of their hands while they'd count to three and swing him up off the ground, making him laugh.

Good times that hadn't lasted, he thought wryly. Within a year, his world had fallen apart when they'd first separated and then divorced. He could still remember the bitterness of their fights, especially because he happened to be at the center of each disagreement.

He'd gone back and forth between his parents' homes for thirteen months, until his mother married James Wallace. Once she gave birth to Brady, Quinn began spending longer and longer time frames with his dad, rather than with his mother and her new family. Eventually, at the age of thirteen, he lived with his father full-time.

Quinn shook off the painful memories as he pulled up to the Life-Everlasting Chapel. Obviously, going to church as a family all those years ago hadn't prevented his parents' marriage from falling apart.

But then again, his father had chosen a path far from God, especially over the last few years of his life when he'd turned to alcohol for comfort. So maybe that wasn't a surprise after all.

His mother, his stepfather and Ivy were already seated inside, talking to the funeral director when he walked in. The place reeked heavily of roses, to the point he had to fight back the urge to sneeze.

He approached the table where his family was seated, feeling invisible when they didn't so much as glance in his direction after he took a seat across from them.

"Just wait here a few moments, and I'll gather everything together for you, all right?" The middle-aged bald funeral director stood, and then when he caught sight of Quinn, quickly introduced himself. "Arthur Crandon," he said in a low, respectfully hushed voice, even as he pulled a business card from his pocket.

"Quinn Murphy," he said in response. "Brady was my half brother."

"My condolences for your loss," Arthur murmured.

"Thanks."

When the funeral director left the room, his mother finally looked at him. "Well?" she demanded. "Do you have any news? Have the police found Brady's killer?"

"No, I'm afraid not." He glanced helplessly

at his stepfather, James Wallace, who sat with a supportive arm around his mother's shoulders. "I don't have anything new to report right now, but the investigation is still ongoing. Hopefully we'll know something soon."

His mother's expression grew angry. "Tell me this, Quinn. What good is it having you on the campus police force if you can't keep my children safe?" she asked harshly.

Resentment swelled in his chest, but he wrestled it back with an effort. His mother's eyes were red and swollen from crying, as were Ivy's. The deep grooves in his stepfather's face and the dark circles under his eyes made him look much older, too. Quinn had seen enough grieving families to know that they often lashed out in anger.

Yet listening to his mother lashing out at him personally hurt more than he'd expected.

"I'm sorry," Quinn repeated. Time to change the subject. He looked at the paperwork Arthur had left on the table. "Is there something I can do? Do you need anything?"

"No, we've already made all the arrangements," his mother said bitterly. "And it doesn't matter anyway, since everything is on hold until after the autopsy." She made the statement another accusation, glaring at him again, as if it were personally his fault that Brady's autopsy wasn't completed yet. And guiltily, he remembered promising her he'd follow up, but he hadn't.

"I'll make some phone calls, see what I can find out about the timeline for releasing Brady's body for the funeral," he said, standing up and reaching for his cell phone. The autopsy should be either in process or almost completed, and hopefully the detective assigned to the case would know the details.

His mother turned to his stepfather and Ivy, effectively dismissing him. For a moment he stood awkwardly, realizing he was only making his relationship with his mother worse by staying. By trying to be a part of the family.

Because he wasn't part of the family. She'd made that clear over the years. Her new family, James, Brady and Ivy, had been the center of her world for a long time.

Once again, he suspected his mother would have preferred to be planning his funeral rather than Brady's. She'd resented him from the very beginning of the divorce, arguing over the forced joint custody arrangements.

Obviously, nothing had changed since then.

"I'll be in touch when I have news," he murmured helplessly before turning and walking back outside.

Taking a deep breath of fresh air to clear the

cloying scent of roses from his nasal passages, he tipped his head back to stare at the crescent-shaped moon surrounded by bright stars in the sky.

If there was a God, he could sure use some help from Him now, he thought idly.

He took another deep breath and glanced down at his phone. After punching in the number for Hank Nelson, he waited for the detective to answer his call.

But, of course, there was no response—from either God or Hank Nelson.

He snapped his phone shut and decided there was plenty of time to do a little investigating of his own before he needed to pick up Shanna. He knew a little about his younger brother, and that one of his favorite hangouts was a small coffee shop located not far from his house.

His mother deserved answers, and he was more determined than ever to get them for her.

It was the least he could do, after the way he'd messed up her life.

Shanna rubbed at her burning eyes and gave up, pushing away from the computer screen. The images were so blurry, she couldn't trust herself to continue. What if she missed Skylar simply because of exhaustion and eyestrain?

No, better to head home and begin again tomorrow, when her vision would be fresh and crisp.

She stood and gathered her jacket and her purse. Spying her cell phone, she picked it up and then hesitated.

Should she call Quinn? Or not?

Glancing at her watch, she realized she'd been sitting in front of the computer reviewing photos for almost two hours. Was Quinn still busy making funeral arrangements? She had no idea how long something like that would take.

She glanced at the phone and scrolled through it. No missed text message or phone calls that she could see. So he hadn't called her. The flash of disappointment was completely illogical. Quinn was likely still in the midst of planning his brother's funeral.

There was no reason to bother him for something as simple and basic as a ride home when she could just as easily call for a cab. Quinn should be supporting his family during a difficult time like this.

She called for a cab and then went outside to wait for her ride. The crisp October air had turned cool and she burrowed down in her coat, seeking warmth. Just when she was about to go back inside the building to wait, her cab came around the corner and parked near the curb.

Glancing at her cell phone one last time to verify there were no calls from Quinn, she tucked it in her pocket and slid into the backseat of the cab. She gave the driver her address and then settled back for the short ride.

She lived on the southwest side of Chicago, and the ride from Carlyle University only took about fifteen minutes. She paid the driver in cash and climbed out of the cab.

Her house was completely dark, and Shanna realized she must have forgotten to leave the kitchen light on as she usually did. Was it only this morning that she'd found out about Skylar's fingerprints? Seemed as if the phone call from Al had taken place twelve days ago.

She paused at the mailbox and opened it cautiously, hoping there wasn't another mysteriously blank, threatening note inside. When she didn't find anything but a handful of junk mail, her shoulders sagged in relief.

Thank You, Lord.

The whispered prayer felt good, felt right after not talking to God for so long. She couldn't believe she'd given up on her faith. With a small smile, she tucked the junk mail under her arm and searched inside her purse for her house keys as she walked up to the front door.

Maybe it was time to try calling her father

again. Not to tell him about Skylar—she wanted to have better news first. But she could keep trying to mend the rift between them. The crime scene she'd worked just after the Markoviack case was also related to a brutal murder. And the victim's sister kept going on and on about how they hadn't spoken in years, and now it was too late. She'd immediately gone home to call her father, leaving several messages, but her father hadn't answered her calls. She'd even gone so far as to show up at his apartment, but he'd looked out the window, saw her and then refused to answer the door.

She knew her father blamed her for Skylar's disappearance, but she'd hoped he'd eventually let go of his anger. Yet it was difficult to make amends when he wouldn't even give her a chance to talk.

When the victim's sister had confessed how they hadn't spoken to each other in over a year, Shanna had been able to relate. Because her father hadn't spoken to her in over ten years. And she was ashamed to admit she hadn't tried to get in touch with him until recently.

Maybe mending their relationship was hopeless, but it wouldn't be her decision to give up. Not this time. No matter what, she intended to keep trying.

With a sigh, she unlocked the front door and

walked inside. She paused for a moment to allow her eyes to adjust to the darkness. A loud creak echoed through the house, and she froze in the act of reaching for the light switch.

Was someone inside?

Shanna stayed exactly where she was, straining to listen. But now, all she heard was silence.

Slowly, the tension in her muscles eased. The noise must have been her imagination. Or just the normal creaks and groans of an older home.

She swept her hand along the wall, searching for and finding the light switch. She flipped the lever up.

Nothing.

With a frown, she flipped it on and off again. Still no light flashed on.

What were the odds that both lightbulbs in both lamps would go out at the exact same time?

Probably about the same as finding her missing sister's fingerprints at a crime scene.

As she was about to make her way across the room, she smelled some sort of heavy aftershave just a fraction of a second before she heard another rustling sound.

Someone was inside! The stalker!

Instinctively she ducked to the side, toward the door, in a desperate move to escape.

But she was too late. She felt a hand clamp down onto her arm seconds before pain exploded in the back of her head.

FIVE

Quinn called Shanna's cell phone for the fifth time, frowning when, once again, the call went unanswered. Hadn't they agreed she'd wait for him? Granted, he'd stayed at the coffeehouse, which had been unusually packed with college kids for a Monday night, longer than he'd anticipated. But still, they'd had an agreement.

When he didn't find Shanna in the computer library, his annoyance grew. Why wasn't she answering his calls? The hour wasn't that late—if she had gone home, she could have at least told him her plans. Or answer her phone.

She acted as if there was no reason to fear the weirdo guy leaving threatening messages.

The itch along the back of his neck wouldn't go away, so Quinn headed to her house, on the southwest side of town. He pushed the speed limit, figuring he'd use his badge to get out of a ticket if he was stopped.

He pulled up in front of Shanna's house, scowling when he noticed the place was completely dark. Was it possible she'd really gone to bed by eight-thirty at night?

Or hadn't she gotten home yet?

He climbed out of his car and approached the front door, knowing that if she had gone to bed, she wouldn't be thrilled to find him standing there.

He hesitated, but then shook his head. Too bad. He wasn't leaving without talking to her. With a determined stride, he stepped up on the porch and knocked loudly on the door.

No answer. He knocked again, harder. When she still didn't respond, he tried the door handle. To his surprise, it wasn't locked. Warily, he pulled his weapon from his shoulder holster and flattened himself against the wall before pushing the front door open.

The door didn't open all the way, and it took him a moment to realize there was something in the way. Pale skin, gleaming in the moonlight. An outstretched hand.

Shanna?

With his heart pounding in his chest, he quickly dialed 911, knowing he needed backup—and fast.

"What's the nature of your emergency?" the dispatcher asked.

"I have an injured woman, and her attacker could still be on the premises," he said urgently, keeping his voice as low as possible. He quickly rattled off her address. "Send the police and an ambulance. Hurry!"

The dispatcher told him to wait outside for the police, but he ignored her. Setting his phone on the ground to keep the connection, he decided there was no way he was going to sit there and do nothing when Shanna was hurt. He had no way of knowing if the intruder was still inside, so he eased through the narrow opening, keeping his back to the wall.

The house was quiet, but that didn't mean anything. The person could still be inside, waiting for him. Quinn swept his hand up for the light switch, and the itch on the back of his neck intensified when the lights didn't come on.

Keeping his weapon ready, he slid down the wall and reached out to feel for a pulse. Overwhelming relief swept over him when his fingers found the faint beat of her heart.

Thank You, God.

The prayer flashing into his mind was a surprise, as was the calming sense of peace. He didn't have time to dwell on it, though. Instead, he continued to listen for any indication that the prowler was still around, knowing her house was an unsecured crime scene.

Every instinct he had screamed at him to get Shanna out of there. But he was afraid to move her. Keeping his weapon ready, he gently used his free hand to check for injuries.

Shanna was lying facedown, as if she'd tried to run for the door. And as he swept a hand over her hair, he found the sticky wetness at the base of her skull that could only be blood.

His stomach twisted with fear. *Please, God, keep her safe.* Wishing desperately for some light, he once again debated his options. Move her? Or wait for backup to arrive?

What could possibly be taking the ambulance so long to get here? And the police? Hadn't those two cops promised to drive past Shanna's house on a regular basis?

There were no indications anyone was still in the house, but the perpetrator could be hiding. Waiting. He wasn't leaving Shanna's side. Not until he knew for sure she was safe.

The wail of sirens finally reached his ears, but he didn't relax until he could hear the thuds of police boots on the step.

"Quinn Murphy, campus police," he said, announcing his presence. "I'm here beside the injured victim, but I haven't been able to confirm the house is secure."

"Okay. The ambulance is here, but we're going to do a sweep of the house first."

Quinn understood the need for safety, and he continued his vigilance next to Shanna while the rest of the Chicago P.D. went through the house.

"Kitchen, clear!"

"Bathroom, clear!"

"Bedroom one, clear!"

"Master bedroom, clear!"

The officers went through the entire house, including the basement, and then suddenly, the living room lights came on. The bright light was so unexpected, Quinn winced and ducked his head, trying to blink away the sudden blindness.

Seeing Shanna in the light did not reassure him. Her hair was matted with blood. Too much blood.

"Someone turned the breaker off," one of the officers said when he returned to the living room.

When the EMTs arrived, Quinn reluctantly moved out of the way, giving them room to work. Shanna groaned when they gently logrolled her onto a backboard, and then lifted her up onto the stretcher.

"What happened?" she asked, wincing as she raised a hand to her head.

"You tell us," Quinn said, taking her hand in

his, needing the connection. He could hardly relax; adrenaline still rushed through his bloodstream a million miles a minute. "Looks like someone hit you on the back of the head."

"Yes," she whispered, her blue eyes clinging to his. "Someone was in my house. I tried to get away…" her voice trailed off.

"It's okay," he said reassuringly. He was just so glad to see her awake. And talking, in spite of the copious amount of blood. "Don't worry, you're going to be okay."

"Quinn, I'm sorry," she said, as her eyelids fluttered closed. "I should have waited."

"Don't apologize," he said again. This wasn't the time to argue. Not when her face was still so pale, and the tension around her mouth and eyes indicated she was in pain. All that mattered right now was knowing she'd be okay.

But he couldn't deny being concerned about the extent of her head injury.

"Which hospital are you taking her to?" he asked, as the EMTs loaded her into the back of the ambulance.

"Hospital?" she squeaked, her luminous blue eyes opening wide. "I'm fine! Just give me a few minutes to gather my thoughts. I don't need to go to the hospital."

Now he was going to argue. Big-time. "You're going to the hospital, Shanna. End of discussion."

The EMTs gaped at his harsh tone, and then the one closest to Shanna's head glanced down at her. "He's right," the EMT said kindly. "You really need to be checked out. The doctors are going to want a CT scan of your head to make sure there's no internal bleeding."

"Which hospital?" he asked again, impatiently.

"Chicago Central. It's the closest."

"I'll meet you there." He watched Shanna for a few seconds, relieved when she gave up and relaxed back on the gurney. He closed the ambulance door and then turned back to the cops swarming around Shanna's house. "What did you find?" he asked.

"Nothing resembling a weapon," the older cop said grumpily. His name tag identified him as Officer Rawlings. "We'll have the place dusted for prints, but whatever he used to hit her on the back of the head, he took with him."

Quinn couldn't help but agree. "Anything else?"

"We found her cell phone." Rawlings raised a brow. "Looks as if you called her several times."

He glanced at her phone display, where she'd labeled his cell number with his name. "Yeah, well she wasn't supposed to come home alone." He was bothered by the way she hadn't waited for him. Didn't she trust him? He said he'd return. "She was supposed to wait for me. There's been some wacky guy following her, leaving threatening notes."

"Yeah, I saw a copy of the report." Rawlings chomped hard on a piece of gum. "Good thing for you. Otherwise we'd be taking you downtown for a chat."

Quinn felt his temper rise, and he had to take a calming breath before responding. These guys were only doing their jobs, even if they weren't doing them very well, at least in his opinion. "I'm not the assailant who's been stalking her. I was at the Corner Café Coffee Shop between six and eight tonight. Plenty of people can verify that I was there."

"Okay," Rawlings agreed mildly. "We'll check out your alibi. No reason to get your boxers in a bundle."

He let that one slide. "Have you figured out how the assailant got inside?"

"Yep. There's a broken window in the basement we think he used to gain entry. We suspect he tripped the breaker and then hunkered down to wait for Ms. Dawson to come home. I suppose you're going to want to see everything for yourself?"

He did, but he wanted even more to make

sure Shanna was okay. "Later. Right now, I'm heading to Chicago Central."

Shanna kept her eyes closed as a halfhearted attempt to minimize the pounding in her head. Her stomach churned with nausea, but she didn't say anything to the EMTs, hoping the sick feeling in her stomach was from knowing someone had been inside her house, and not from a potential brain injury.

She owed Quinn an apology. He'd told her to wait for him but she hadn't, too proud, too stubborn to call him. The excuses seemed flimsy now. She couldn't believe he hadn't said those famous last words.

I told you so.

Of course, saying something like that didn't seem to be Quinn's style.

"Ms. Dawson, we've arrived at the hospital." The EMT loomed over her, fussing with the IV line that they'd placed in her arm. "How are you feeling?" he asked.

"I'm fine." Or at least she would be, once her mammoth-size headache went away.

She couldn't help wincing a bit when they jostled her, pulling the gurney out of the back of the ambulance. As they went in through the emergency department doors, she felt like a complete fraud when a group of staff members rushed over to greet them as if she were on death's door.

"Vitals stable, BP 110/60, pulse 98 and respirations 16," the EMT announced as they wheeled her inside. "She has an open laceration in the back of her head, and was found unconscious at the scene."

Good heavens, the EMT was making her sound far worse than she was. "I'm fine," she said, trying to make eye contact with one of the staff members.

But it was no use. No one was listening to her, too intent on doing whatever medical tasks they deemed necessary. One nurse hooked her up to a heart monitor, while another checked her blood pressure again. A third one tied a tourniquet around her arm. "Tiny pinch here," she said mere seconds before inserting the needle.

The pain in her head must be bad, since she didn't feel the needle in her vein at all.

"Hi there, my name is Dr. Lyons." A man old enough to be her father bent over her bedside and flashed a kind smile. "I'm just going to take a listen to your heart and lungs for a moment. Then we'll review the extent of your injuries."

The extent of her injuries? "It's just my head," she protested. But she needn't have bothered since no one was paying any attention. The kindly doctor put his stethoscope buds in his ears and listened intently.

Despite being completely surrounded by hospital staff, she'd never felt more alone.

She closed her eyes and tried not to feel sorry for herself. She should be grateful they were all intent on doing their jobs. The sooner she was medically cleared, the sooner she'd be able to go home.

"Shanna?" Quinn's familiar deep voice made her heart jump. She braved the light, opening her eyes to look for him.

"Sorry, sir, you can't be in here," one of the nurses said, putting an arm out to stop him. "No family allowed."

She had to smile when he scowled and flashed his badge. "Police. Ms. Dawson is a victim of a crime."

The nurse relaxed and waved him past. "You can't question her now, so stay out of the way until after we're finished examining her."

Quinn came closer, careful not to interfere with the medical team. "How are you holding up?" he asked in a low voice.

"Better now that you're here." The honest statement slipped out before she could stop it.

His features softened, and when the doctor stepped back he inched a little closer, managing to stay out of the nurse's way even as he reached over to take her hand.

Gratefully, she closed her fingers around his.

For a moment their gazes locked. Held. The depth of emotion in his expression startled her. Tears pricked her eyes, but she told herself they were because of her pounding head, and not just because she was so glad to see him.

"You're going to be fine," he said. And she wondered which of them he was trying to convince.

Within minutes, though, the staff members who'd hovered around her moved on to other tasks. Obviously, she wasn't hurt very badly, since only one nurse remained at her bedside.

"We're going to take you over to radiology in a few minutes, as Dr. Lyons has ordered a CT scan of your head to rule out a subdural hematoma."

A what? Sounded like something bad, so she didn't bother to ask. "Okay."

"I'd like to go with her," Quinn said. Now that everyone had dispersed, no one seemed to mind that he'd planted himself right next to her.

"Fine with me," the nurse said with a shrug.

"You don't have to stay," Shanna murmured. "It's my own fault that I'm even here in the first place."

Quinn's eyebrows levered up. "I hardly think

it's your fault someone broke into your house and waited there for you to come home."

She shook her head and then winced as the slightest motion made the hammering in her head nearly unbearable. "No, I mean it's my fault because I didn't call you."

Quinn stared down at their entwined hands for a long second before raising his gaze to hers. "So why didn't you call me?"

"I thought your family probably needed you more than I did." Or at least, more than she should. But she didn't voice that part. "When you didn't call me, I figured you were busy with your family and forgot." Okay, now that just sounded pathetic.

He let out a heavy sigh. "No, Shanna. I wasn't busy with my family. The funeral arrangements were pretty much finished by the time I arrived."

Really? Then where had he been for the hours she'd spent looking at photos? Before she could ask, a tech came over and began disconnecting her from the heart monitor.

"I'm going to wheel you over to radiology. It's right around the corner from the trauma bay. And the scan won't take long, just ten to fifteen minutes. Are you allergic to anything? Iodine? Shellfish?"

"Not that I know of."

"Great." The tech pushed her bed away and, true to his word, Quinn walked right alongside, holding her hand the entire time. Once she was taken into the scanner he had to step back. But as soon as it was complete, he returned and took her hand again.

This time, the radiology tech took her to a private room. "You've been cleared from a trauma perspective," one of the nurses explained. "We're waiting for the resident to come over to clean and stitch up your scalp laceration."

Didn't that sound like fun? Not. Still, she didn't complain. The resident showed up a moment later. "Good news. Your CT scan is negative, which means you have a minor concussion but no bleeding into your brain. The laceration you have back there is going to need a few stitches, though. Once we're finished with that, you'll be able to go home."

Her stomach lurched at the word *home.*

Stop it, she chided herself. She was lucky to have escaped with only a minor injury. And at least she had a home to go to. Closing her eyes, she offered up a quick prayer. *Thank You for sparing me from greater harm, Lord.*

She slowly turned over so the resident could wash and suture her head. She kept as still as possible, while he first shaved the hair away from the wound and then began to clean it. Her head pounded so badly, she couldn't bring herself to care when she saw long strands of her hair falling to the floor. Apparently, she was going to have a bald spot on the back of her head for a while.

Could have been so much worse.

"More good news, this only needed four stitches," the resident announced cheerfully. "I'm all finished. Just rest here for a few minutes while we get your discharge paperwork ready."

After she rolled over on her back, she caught Quinn's serious gaze. His hand tightened on hers. "You're not going back home alone, Shanna."

"You never mentioned how he got inside."

"Broke in through the basement window and tripped the fuse so the lights wouldn't work. Unfortunately, we didn't find what he used to hit you with."

The force of the blow had felt like a rock, but, honestly, it could have been anything. The thought of staying in her house alone wasn't the least bit appealing, but it would be inappropriate to have Quinn stay with her. "I was thinking about going to a motel for the night."

He looked as if he wanted to argue, but then nodded. "All right, that seems like a reasonable compromise."

"Why do you think he left me alive?" The question had been nagging at her, even though it was hard to imagine anyone hating her enough to hurt her. But why hadn't he made sure she was dead before he left?

Quinn blew out a heavy breath. "Best I can figure, the ringing of your cell phone scared him off. I started calling you, over and over again. Maybe he figured I was closer than I was."

His theory made sense. "Thank you for calling," she whispered. "You probably saved my life."

"I should have called you sooner," he said, his tone full of self-reproach. "So, really, it's my fault you're here. I got caught up in the investigation and lost track of time."

The investigation into Brady's murder? Her attention was diverted from her incessant headache. "Did you find something? Any evidence?"

"Not evidence, exactly," Quinn said slowly. "But one of Brady's roommates told me my brother hung out at the Corner Café Coffee Shop, so I went over there. I flashed his photo and just about everyone remembered Brady being there often."

"Really?"

"Yeah. Several kids told me he was always working on his laptop computer, using the free Wi-Fi services the coffee shop provided. I assumed he was probably doing homework of some sort. Until one person mentioned Brady's article."

She frowned. "Article? What sort of article?"

"I'm not sure," he admitted. "But I did a little digging and discovered Brady was taking a journalism course. He was also one of the reporters for the college's online newspaper."

She didn't quite understand why this news was so important. "So what does that mean? I'm sure there are a lot of kids who are journalism majors."

"Yeah, but this one kid I spoke to seemed to think Brady was hot on some story. Some story he was pretty secretive about. I'm just wondering if he stumbled into something he shouldn't have."

She stared at Quinn, unable to imagine what sort of information a college student could stumble upon that was bad enough to get him killed.

SIX

Shanna seemed surprised by his revelation, but they were interrupted when the gum-chewing Officer Rawlings entered Shanna's hospital room. Quinn frowned. "Did you find something significant?"

"No." Rawlings crossed over to the other side of Shanna's bed. "Ms. Dawson, we'd like you to go through your home to inventory anything that might be missing."

"Missing?" Shanna's alabaster skin paled even more. "Do you think the intruder was trying to rob me?"

Quinn snorted his disbelief, but Rawlings ignored him. "We want to cover all possibilities. It doesn't look like much has been disturbed, but you'd be the best one to judge for sure. Here's my card. I'd like you to call me once you're finished."

Shanna seemed upset by the news. "All right."

Quinn took the card from Shanna's fingers and

tucked it into his breast pocket. "I'll be sure she makes a list if anything's missing."

Rawlings shrugged. "Fine." He turned to Shanna. "I need a statement from you, Ms. Dawson, and I'd rather get the details while they're fresh in your mind."

"Okay," she responded.

"Tell me what happened, starting with where you were before you went home." Rawlings pulled out a small notebook and a stubby pencil, glancing at her expectantly.

"I spent most of the day at Carlyle University. I called for a cab about ten minutes to eight at night. The cabbie arrived about five minutes later, and I probably got home around eight-fifteen or so."

Quinn tightened his grip on her hand. Five minutes. He'd missed her at Carlyle University by five minutes!

"Then what happened?" Rawlings asked.

"I came home and went in through the front door. I'm not sure why," she mused with a frown, "because normally I go inside through the side door."

"Hmm." Rawlings jotted something down in his notebook.

"I thought I heard something, but figured it

was just the normal creaks and groans of an older house. I flipped on the light switch, but it didn't work."

"Then what happened?"

She hesitated, her fingers tightening around his. "I smelled him." Rawlings's eyebrows rose upward. "I know that sounds crazy, but he was wearing some sort of stinky aftershave. The moment I realized I wasn't alone, I tried to run, but he hit me on the back of the head."

Listening to Shanna reiterate the series of events wasn't easy. He should have been there with her.

"Anything else? Did you see him at all?"

"No. I only smelled him."

Rawlings shut his notebook. "Okay, if you think of anything else, give me a call."

"I will." Shanna's smile was strained.

Quinn waited until after Rawlings left. "If we went to the store to test samples of aftershave, would you be able to pinpoint what he smelled like?"

She wrinkled her nose. "Yes. I'm sure I'd recognize it."

Satisfied they might have at least one lead, he nodded. "Okay, plan on going tomorrow, then."

"I need to look at more photos of college students tomorrow," she protested. "We'll check out the aftershave later."

"There's no guarantee your sister is enrolled at the university," he pointed out.

"It's my best lead," she repeated stubbornly.

They were interrupted by the resident coming back into Shanna's room. "Here you go. Here's a prescription for a narcotic pain reliever, although it might be helpful to start with over-the-counter medication like ibuprofen first." He went through the list of discharge instructions, stressing the importance of coming back to the hospital if her symptoms got any worse.

"Sign here." The resident indicated the paperwork.

She signed and then swung her legs over the side of the bed. She swayed a bit, and Quinn reached out a hand to steady her.

"Which motel?" he asked as she slowly made her way outside. He steered her in the direction of his car.

"Quinn, I want to go home first."

Home? "I thought we'd reached a compromise."

Her face took on the all-too-familiar stubborn expression. "Home, so I can check for anything missing and pack an overnight case."

"Home first, then a motel," he agreed reluctantly.

She slid into the passenger seat and kept her

eyes closed during the short ride back to her house. He glanced at her frequently, wondering if he should just ignore her desire to get whatever she needed and take her straight to the motel.

She had to be exhausted. Not that he blamed her. But the moment he pulled into her driveway, her eyes opened. "Are you sure you're all right?" he asked.

"As fine as I can be with a monster headache," she said with a wry smile. She pulled out her keys. "Guess I should get my locks changed."

"At the very least." He came around to help her out of the car. "I thought you were considering a security system?"

"I have to admit, that idea is sounding better and better." She went in through the side door this time, walking into the kitchen. He followed her inside, glanced around curiously. The interior of her house was neat, tidy.

"Give me a few minutes to look around and then pack my things," she said, moving down the hall, flipping lights on as she went, making her way toward the bedrooms.

Quinn stood in the kitchen, glancing around curiously. Had the intruder waited for her in here? Only to be disappointed when she came in the front door instead?

There weren't a lot of hiding places, though.

The kitchen table was tucked into a corner, and the rest of the kitchen area was wide open, with the white cabinets mounted on two walls across from the entryway.

He walked over behind the door to mimic what the intruder might have done. The assailant had waited right here for her to come in, holding his weapon—a bat, or a club of some sort—ready in his hand.

How long had he waited? Ten minutes? Thirty? A couple of hours? The assailant had chosen to lie in wait for her, rather than to follow her.

Next time you'll be alone.

The last note she'd received mocked him, and he battled a wave of guilt. Next time, she wouldn't be alone.

Standing with his back against the wall, he imagined how the assailant must have heard Shanna come in through the front door. Waiting in the dark, having tripped the breakers in the fuse box, meant he must have felt along the wall, moving toward the opening to make his way into the living room.

Quinn took the path that made the most sense, and right at the entryway into the living area, a floorboard creaked under his weight.

Bingo.

The satisfaction was bittersweet. Thankfully,

Shanna had come in through the front door. Because if she'd come in through the kitchen, her assailant might have killed her.

But because he'd had to move through the house, she'd heard him and smelled him, which caused her to run for the door. Maybe in the dark, the assailant had misjudged the distance and hadn't hit her as hard as he'd intended. And then Quinn had called her cell phone several times, one call right after the other, scaring the guy off.

The scenario he'd created fit. Only too well.

Grimly, Quinn turned and headed for the basement. Rawlings had told him the guy had come in through a broken window. The least he could do while he waited was secure the house.

But when he flipped on the basement light, he was surprised to discover one of the officers on scene had already done the work. A board was nailed securely over the broken window, and the shards of glass had been swept into a neat pile.

Thoughtfully, he walked back upstairs. Glancing at his watch, he wondered what was taking her so long. "Shanna? Do you have everything you need?"

"Not yet," came her muffled reply. From where he stood, at the beginning of the hallway, he could tell her voice came from the bedroom closer to him, not the master bedroom, which was further down the hall.

He didn't think this was the right time to go through her stuff to make sure nothing was stolen. Rawlings was crazy if he thought this was the work of a burglar. He'd bet his entire pension that the stalker who'd left the threatening notes was the guy who'd waited patiently for her in the kitchen.

He headed down the hallway. "Shanna, we need to leave," he said, pausing in the doorway of the first bedroom. She used it as an office, judging by the rolltop desk and computer taking up one wall. He found her half-buried inside the closet. "What are you looking for?"

She didn't answer, but he could hear her mumbling to herself. "It's here somewhere. I know it is."

What was there somewhere? "Let me help you look," he offered, venturing farther into the room.

"You can't help me. I'm the one who put it somewhere safe. Or so I thought." After another few minutes, she finally exclaimed, "I found it!"

He watched as she pulled a large box down from a shelf in the back of the closet, staggering a little beneath the weight. Before he could take it from her, she set it on the floor and dropped to her knees. Gently, she pried off the lid, and the first item he saw was a pink stuffed elephant.

This was what she was searching for? His stomach twisted. Maybe her head injury was worse than they'd thought. "Shanna, come on, we really need to get you to a motel room. I think you need to get some rest."

She lifted her gaze to his, and the tortured expression in her luminous blue eyes tugged at his heart. "I couldn't leave without making sure everything was still here."

Everything? A pink stuffed animal? And then he understood. "These are Skylar's personal belongings, aren't they?"

"Yes." Shanna rifled through the box. "Most of it is Skylar's—a few of her stuffed animals, her baby ring, her favorite blanket. But I also have my research notes in here from the investigation."

"Investigation?" His curiosity piqued, he came over to kneel beside her. He wished Rawlings had never given her the idea this could be the work of a burglar. "The police investigation?"

"Not exactly." She rocked back on her heels. "My own investigation. Skylar's kidnapping is what made me decide to go into CSI work in the first place, and I never gave up hope that we'd eventually find out what happened to her.

I've continued to work on her case, on and off, for the past eight years."

Shanna knew Quinn was looking at her as if she'd lost her marbles. But what did he expect? Of course she hadn't given up on the cold-case investigation.

"Did you really think the person who broke into your house was here to steal this stuff?" he asked.

"Maybe." How could she explain her convoluted feelings? "Probably not, but I wanted to be sure."

Quinn's gaze was serious. "You told me the notes began to show up a couple of weeks ago, right?" When she nodded, he continued, "So I'm sure Brady's murder and finding your sister's fingerprints at the crime scene aren't connected to the assailant."

Logically, she knew he was right. "I know." She stared down at the box, the sick feeling in her stomach intensifying as she stared at Ellie, the elephant. Skylar's elephant. From what she could see, everything was still there.

"Unless…" Quinn frowned. "Have you been working on your sister's case recently? Interviewing people? Stirring up the past in a way that you're making someone nervous?"

She let out a heavy sigh. "No, I haven't done

any investigating of my sister's case in months." And she was ashamed that she'd let her work cases sidetrack her from finding her sister.

Quinn's expression was full of disappointment. "Okay, then I really don't see how they could possibly be related. Why don't you put this stuff away for now? I think you need to get some rest."

Now that she had the box of her sister's belongings in hand, she was loathe to let it go. Losing the contents of this box would be like losing her sister all over again.

With a sigh, she picked up the folder containing her notes and a stack of newspaper clippings. Several items slid out onto the floor, and she reached over to gather them back together.

"Wait a minute," Quinn said, putting his hand on hers. He picked up the article closest to him and scanned the newspaper print. "This isn't related to Skylar's kidnapping. It's about some other child."

"Yeah, I know." When he still looked puzzled, she tried to explain. "There weren't many clues about Skylar's disappearance. I got a copy of the police report, and none of the people interviewed had seen anything. So I searched on the internet for other cases that were similar to Skylar's."

"Other cases," he repeated. "In the Chicago area?"

"Not just in the Chicago area," she explained.

"But I did find about six other cases that all took place in an eighteen-month time frame and within a hundred-mile radius."

Quinn looked totally shocked. "That's incredible. I think you were clearly onto something, Shanna. But I can't figure out why the feds weren't involved?"

"They were for a while. They interviewed my parents. But other than that, I don't know that they found out much, probably because each case was slightly different." She pulled out several of the articles showing what she meant. "See this child here? His father disappeared at the same time, and the parents were divorced, so the crime was considered to be the result of the custody battle."

"But they never found the father or the child?" Quinn persisted.

"No." At his skeptical gaze, she shrugged. "I know it's odd, but they figured the guy must have gone to Mexico, or maybe Canada."

"Interesting." He shuffled through the articles to pick up another one. "Wow, this child is just fourteen months old."

"Yeah, that one wasn't exactly like the other children. Most of the ages were between two and a half and five. My sister was one of the oldest children taken."

"The FBI must have a file on this," Quinn

mused, his gaze sweeping over all the evidence she'd collected over the years. "Maybe now that we have Skylar's prints at the crime scene we should call them."

"You're probably right," she agreed slowly. With the FBI's resources, surely they'd have the ability to track down Skylar better than she could. If they were even willing to reopen the case. Surely finding Skylar's fingerprints gave them a good reason.

"I know I'm right." Quinn sat down on the floor next to her box, making himself comfortable. She smiled, realizing his cop instincts had gotten the better of him. Now that he knew there might be other missing children related to Skylar's case, he was intrigued by the information.

"Hey, this kid was taken from a shopping mall," Quinn said, a note of eagerness in his voice. "That's pretty similar to being taken from a school."

"I know. That was the case I spent the most time on because the cases were so similar." She leaned in to read over his shoulder, even though she had the details of the article memorized. "The only difference was that Kenny was a boy, and just a month shy of being four years old."

She remembered the case all too well. Kenny Larson was the child who'd been taken, nearly nine months before Skylar. The nearly four-year-old had been at the mall with his grandmother when they'd gotten separated. Thinking he was lost, his grandmother had frantically called the mall security, and they'd gone through every store. Finally, suspecting the worst, they reviewed every mall exit security tape but, despite their efforts, had not been able to capture a photo of the kidnapper.

She remembered because there was a long article about how the police had an image they were working with, a large group of people leaving the mall at the same time with a small boy in the middle of the group. But the image was so blurry and the group so large, that even with skilled enhancements, they hadn't been able to pinpoint the kidnapper.

"You know, maybe we should take this stuff with us to the motel," Quinn admitted. "If nothing else, we could spend some time reviewing the evidence, see if anything jumps out at us."

"We?" she echoed, pouncing on the pronoun. "Quinn, you're not staying in the motel room with me."

He merely raised a brow. "Are you telling me I can't check into a room right next to yours?" he asked carefully. "Because I'm pretty sure they'll give out rooms to anyone willing to pay for one."

She bit her lip, forced to admit she'd love nothing more than to have Quinn be in a motel room right next door to her. But she was already leaning on him far too much.

What would happen when Brady's murder investigation was over? And they'd found her sister? Each of them would end up going their separate ways.

Quinn was just being nice and supportive to her because he was a cop, and she happened to be in danger. He'd held her hand throughout her brief hospital stay because he was a nice guy and he felt responsible for the attack. He wasn't attracted to her.

Not the same way she was attracted to him.

Besides, she wasn't in the market for a relationship. She wasn't very good at them, anyway. At least, according to Garrett, the one relationship she'd had during college.

"Obviously you can do whatever you'd like, Quinn," she said finally, raising her gaze to his. "But be honest. I'm sure you have other things you'd rather be doing, like following up on more leads related to Brady's murder."

He gave a careless shrug, but she could tell she'd hit a nerve. "In helping you find Skylar, I could also uncover a lead related to Brady's murder. And besides," he hesitated and then reached over to take her hand, "I need to know you're safe."

His confession touched her in the deepest recesses of her soul. When was the last time she'd ever felt as if someone was on her side?

Ducking her head to hide her blush, she quickly gathered the articles together. "Okay, then let's go."

In her haste, she moved too quickly, and several documents slid out of the folder. Feeling even more foolish for the slightest betrayal of her nervousness, she quickly gathered them back together. Her gaze landed on Skylar's birth certificate.

She froze, staring down at the date in complete disbelief.

"What's wrong?" Quinn asked, reaching over to lightly grasp her arm. "Is your headache getting worse?"

Slowly she shook her head. How could she have forgotten? The first of September was the day Skylar had disappeared. The date was burned into her brain, had haunted her ever since.

"Shanna, please. Tell me what's wrong."

She finally raised her tortured gaze to his. "I don't know how I missed this, but today is October 19th. Skylar's birthday."

SEVEN

The tiny hairs on the back of Quinn's neck stood on end as he stared at Shanna in shocked surprise. Today was Skylar's birthday?

They'd just decided Shanna's stalker and Skylar's kidnapping couldn't possibly be related, but that was before this bit of news. Was it really a coincidence that Shanna was attacked by her stalker on the day of her missing sister's birthday?

Quinn didn't believe in coincidences.

"You're sure you haven't done any investigating related to your sister's disappearance in the past few months?" he asked again. His gut was clamoring at him, but there had to be a connection somewhere. "Because now that we know today is Skylar's birthday, I can't help thinking there must be some connection between your stalker and your sister's disappearance." It was the only possibility that made sense, even though the timing was off.

Her stalker had started sending notes a couple of weeks ago, and they'd just found her sister's prints two days ago. But the attack on Shanna occurring on Skylar's birthday seemed to be some sort of message.

One they couldn't afford to ignore.

"I'm absolutely sure," Shanna said firmly. "Honestly, Quinn, my job has been so busy over the past few months that I haven't had time." Her gaze dropped to the birth certificate in her hands and her mouth turned down at the corners. "No, that's not quite true. The real answer is that I haven't made time. I allowed my job to take precedence over my sister."

He hated the way she kept beating herself up over this. No matter what she thought, her sister's kidnapping wasn't her fault. "Without some new clue or piece of information to go on, what good would come from reviewing the same old evidence?" he asked reasonably. "Even the feds have pretty much given up the investigation, right?"

"Yeah, maybe," Shanna murmured, sliding the birth certificate back into the folder with the rest of the paperwork. "But giving up on Skylar isn't the answer, either."

He tried to ignore the twinge of guilt. Wasn't he allowing Shanna to distract him from finding Brady's killer? He could pretend that finding her sister might give him a clue to Brady's murder, but he knew that wasn't entirely true. For some odd reason, he wanted to help Shanna.

He did his best to drag his attention back to the matter at hand. "Look, Shanna, you can't change what happened in the past—all you can do is move forward from here. And now we have the best lead ever—your sister's fingerprint at a crime scene, linked to a university." *And a stalker who's watching you,* he added silently.

His words seemed to hit home as she straightened and nodded. "You're right, Quinn. I'd like to take all this stuff with me to the hotel. Going through the evidence again may spark a new idea."

"Sounds like a plan," he agreed. "And I can look at the evidence too at some point. Maybe a new pair of eyes will pick up something you've missed."

"Ah, sure." Again, she seemed flustered by his offer to assist. Because she thought he was becoming too friendly? During those hours at the hospital, she'd clung to his hand as if it were a lifeline. But now she avoided his gaze as she finally put all the items from Skylar's childhood and her investigation into the box. "We'd better get going," she said.

He shouldn't be surprised at how she pulled

away. Hadn't he learned his lesson about relationships after the fiasco with Leslie leaving him? Quinn rose to his feet, taking the box from her hands even though it wasn't very heavy. "Do you have your overnight bag packed?"

"Yes. Give me a minute to get it, and I'll meet you in the kitchen."

He nodded and carried the box out to the kitchen where Shanna met him less than a minute later. He waited until she closed the door and locked it before storing the box and her overnight bag in the back of his SUV.

The ride to the hotel didn't take long, and he even took extra precautions, using a zigzag route to make sure they weren't followed. When he was satisfied no one could possibly have tailed them, he pulled into the parking lot. The chain hotel wasn't anything fancy, and at the last minute, he decided against staying there with her.

Keeping a measure of professional distance between them would be smart. Safe. Shanna was in the middle of a family crisis, and the last thing she needed was to worry about him crowding her. And that wasn't his intention. But surely they could be friends?

And besides, he needed to put more time and effort into investigating Brady's murder. What sort of man let a pretty woman get in the way of his duty? Not Quinn Murphy, that's for sure.

When he requested one room, not two, in the middle of the hallway, halfway between the elevators and stairwells, she glanced at him in surprise but didn't utter a single protest. And she insisted on using her own credit card to foot the bill.

"Thanks for the ride, Quinn," she said, reaching for her overnight bag. Was it his imagination, or was her smile strained? "I appreciate all your help tonight."

He didn't relinquish his hold on her overnight bag or the box of Skylar's things. "I'm not staying because I need to check on my mother. She's really been a wreck over Brady." The excuse sounded weak, even to him. "I'll walk you up to your room," he offered, grasping on to the flimsiest excuse to prolong their time together.

"There's no need," she protested. But he ignored her and walked over to the elevator, punching the button to open the door. She rolled her eyes and crossed her arms over her chest.

During the elevator ride, he racked his brain trying to think of something to say. Something to ease the sudden tension between them.

Something to reassure her that his intentions were honorable.

The elevator doors opened on the third floor,

the highest floor of the midsize hotel, and he followed behind her as she walked briskly to her room.

She unlocked the door and pushed it open, so he could set her bag and box inside. She stayed at the door until he returned. "Thanks again, Quinn," she said.

"You're welcome," he murmured. On the threshold he paused, and then turned back to face her. "Shanna, I know we just met a few days ago, but I hope you consider me a friend. Please call me if you need anything, okay?"

"Of course I consider you a friend, Quinn," she assured him. Was that relief he saw reflected in her eyes? "And I really do appreciate everything you've done for me."

Ridiculous to be disappointed at how quickly she'd accepted his offer of friendship. "Anytime, Shanna." And when it came time to walk away, he simply couldn't do it. "How about meeting me here for lunch tomorrow to compare notes?"

A flicker of surprise flashed across her features. "You're off work again tomorrow?"

"Yeah. They gave me a week off, due to Brady's death." And here he was trying to figure out a way to spend more time with Shanna.

"Okay, lunch tomorrow would be great. Good night, Quinn."

It took every ounce of willpower he had to step back, rather than gathering her close for a hug. "Good night, Shanna."

He waited until she'd closed the door and slid the dead bolt home. Then he forced himself to walk away.

He had six days of vacation/bereavement time off work. It was about time he put forth a stronger effort to find Brady's killer.

And he vowed to start tonight. The customers at the coffee shop thought Brady was working on some "secret" article. There was no easy way to get a hold of Brady's computer tonight, although earlier, he'd put in a second call to Hank Nelson requesting a copy of all the files on Brady's hard drive.

But he could go back through his brother's previous college newsletter articles to see what sorts of topics Brady liked to write about.

And maybe focusing on Brady would make it easier to forget about Shanna, at least for a little while.

Shanna sat down at the desk inside her room and began to review her notes from Skylar's kidnapping. But her throbbing headache wasn't easy to ignore. When she realized she'd read the same paragraph three times and still couldn't remember a word, she shoved the notes aside.

It was no use. She couldn't concentrate.

Turning off the lights and climbing into bed helped to ease the pain a little.

She was exhausted. Mentally and physically exhausted. So why couldn't she sleep?

The image of Quinn's earnest expression as he asked if they could be friends flashed in her mind. She should be glad, relieved that he considered her a friend.

So why the hint of disappointment?

It wasn't as if she and Quinn had a lot in common. Other than maybe being estranged from their respective families.

But Quinn wasn't comfortable talking about God, which should be a huge hint that friendship was all that could ever be between them.

Look what happened when she'd tried to date Garrett? They'd started out as friends, but then he began pushing for a physical relationship when she wasn't ready, and in the end, they'd broken up and their friendship had been ruined.

She didn't want to make the same mistake with Quinn.

Shanna pushed Quinn's image out of her mind and tried to focus on her newly reawakened faith.

Dear Lord, please guide me on Your chosen

path. Help me to find Skylar and please keep my sister safe in Your care. Amen.

The tension eased from her body, lightening the throbbing in her head. But it wasn't until, just as she was falling asleep, that it occurred to her— maybe God intended her to show Quinn the value of believing in God and the power of faith.

When Shanna woke up the next morning, she felt a hundred percent better. Her headache had subsided to nothing more than a dull ache, easily treated with ibuprofen, and her stomach rumbled with hunger, indicating the return of her appetite.

She splurged a little, ordering a light breakfast through room service, mindful of the lunch she'd promised to share later that morning with Quinn.

And after she'd eaten her yogurt parfait and toast, showered and dressed in fresh clothes, she went back to reviewing her notes. But reading through them with the knowledge that Skylar was alive today didn't help shed any light on the events around her kidnapping. Nothing jumped out at her as significant.

After a couple of hours, she sat back in disgust. Going over the scant information in the articles about other kidnapping cases she'd dug out all those years ago wasn't where she should be spending her time or her energy. She needed to be back at Carlyle University going through photographs of female students.

Looking for someone who resembled Skylar.

She glanced at her watch, considering whether or not to cancel the lunch plans with Quinn. If she called for a taxi now, she could easily be back at the university in thirty minutes or less.

But she'd slept later than she'd thought, and Quinn was due to arrive in forty-five minutes. Maybe it would be better for her to spend the time checking on how the processing of evidence was going.

Putting a call in to her forensic expert, Al, she waited on hold until he picked up the call. "Yeah?"

"Hi, Al," she greeted him. "Just wondering how things are going. Did you find any other finger-print matches? Or anything on the hair fibers?"

"We did get a couple of fingerprint matches," he acknowledged. "But all from beer cans, not from the rugby trophy or the victim's room."

Prints off the beer cans didn't mean a whole lot, but at this point, she'd take what they could get. "Okay, give me the names of the matches."

"There is an Erwin Fink, who is in the system because of a shoplifting record as a juvie—he stole a CB radio. And a Bradley Wilkes, whose prints were in the system because he spent four months in the military. Before you start thinking the worst, he was honorably discharged after they discovered a medical problem with his heart that they didn't find during the routine medical screening."

Shanna wrote down the two names, hoping and praying they wouldn't be dead ends. How sad to hope they had some sort of criminal tendency that would make them the logical suspects in Brady's murder. "That's all? Just two matches?"

"Hold on to your horses, would ya?" Al said irritably. "I'm getting to the others. We did match up the three boys who live in the house to prints on beer cans, as well, which isn't a huge surprise. I think it's a little odd that we didn't find any prints of his roommates in the victim's room."

She didn't think that information was so surprising. Living together in a house likely meant they'd spend most of their time in the living room and kitchen, wouldn't they? Not in each other's bedrooms.

"But there are two other names that popped out of the system—Tanya Jacobs and Derek Matthews. I saved these for last because I think they're your best place to start. Both of these kids were in serious trouble last year, and it just so happens they both were busted at the same time."

Her pulse jumped with excitement as she jotted

down the two names, underlining them with bold strokes. "At the same time? What for?"

"Drug dealing on campus." The note of satisfaction in Al's tone was unmistakable.

"At Carlyle University?" she asked in shock. Didn't students get kicked out of school for that sort of criminal activity?

"Interestingly enough, no, they were at a state-college campus in Milwaukee, Wisconsin. They were arrested last year, did only a few months of time before they were released again."

"I can't imagine they're enrolled in college. Wouldn't they do a criminal background check?" she asked. It was interesting that the two kids, male and female, came to Chicago together, once again hanging out with the college crowd. Were they in a romantic relationship? And was their intent to continue dealing drugs?

"Not routinely in the state of Illinois," he told her. "But I haven't checked yet to see if they are enrolled. Figured you could do that part. I knew you'd be interested in these two. Maybe your victim was somehow involved in the drug scene, too?"

Shanna found herself hoping not, for Quinn's sake. "We'll know after we get the autopsy results if he had drugs in his system, in addition to the alcohol."

"Yeah, the preliminary results were released this morning, but they won't have the tox screens done for another four to six weeks."

"I know." The lengthy time frame to receive complete autopsy results was annoying, to say the least. But a necessary evil, if you wanted to rule out any and all possibilities. "Thanks, Al. This gives us a place to start."

"I'll keep you posted if anyone else pops up," he promised.

"I'd appreciate it." She hung up and stared down at the two names of potential suspects: Tanya Jacobs and Derek Matthews.

Finally, they had a decent lead. Clearly the fact that these two were arrested together in Milwaukee last year, and now happened to both be at the same party where a young college student ended up dead, bore further scrutiny.

She could hardly wait to give Quinn the news.

Quinn drove up to the hotel fifteen minutes early. He was too excited by what he'd found to stay away.

In the lobby, he called her cell phone. She answered on the second ring. "Hi, Quinn."

"Hi, Shanna," he responded, knowing his goofy grin stretched from ear to ear. "I know I'm early, but I hope you don't mind."

"No, I don't mind. I have a breakthrough on the case that I'd like to discuss with you, anyway," she said.

His fingers tightened on his phone. She had a breakthrough, too? Maybe between the information they'd both discovered, they'd be able to wrap up this entire murder case sooner rather than later. "Great, I have some news, too."

"Okay, see you in a few minutes."

He snapped his phone shut and paced the foyer in front of the elevators, waiting impatiently. When the elevator dinged and the doors opened, he stepped forward eagerly, but then checked himself.

Back off, Murphy, he told himself. Friends. They were just friends, remember?

"Hi, Quinn," she greeted him warmly. He was surprised to see she had her overnight bag with her, but not the box containing Skylar's things. "I hope you don't mind, but I'm going to need a ride out to the university after lunch, so I can go back to reviewing the college ID photos."

"Of course I don't mind." He reached over to take the overnight bag, surprised to find it felt heavier than last night. "Did you want me to run up and get Skylar's box?"

"No thanks, I managed to jam everything in the overnight bag," she admitted with a shy grin.

"The box was bulky and awkward, so I just put everything in the bag and left the box up in the room."

"You're not planning to check out, are you?" he asked with a frown.

"Yes, I am. But let's fight about that later, okay? First I have something important to tell you."

He didn't want to let the matter drop, but he figured there would be time later to get into the issue. She wasn't safe at her house, that was for sure. But at the moment, he wanted to exchange information. "Let's get seated in the restaurant first, okay?"

She nodded. He approached the hostess and requested a booth in the back for privacy.

After they were seated, they quickly placed their order for burgers and soft drinks. Once the waitress left, Shanna leaned forward. "Okay, you first. Tell me what you found out."

"Remember how I told you that I spent a few hours at the Corner Café showing Brady's picture around?" When she nodded, he continued, "And several students claimed he was working on some sort of secret article for the college online newsletter?"

"Yes. Did you find out what he was working on?" she asked.

"Yep. I called Hank and asked for a copy of all

Brady's files from his laptop computer, and he gave them to me. I started going through them and found the article he'd been working on in the weeks before his death."

"Don't keep me in suspense," Shanna urged. "Tell me what the article was about."

He hoped she wouldn't freak out too much when he told her. "I know this may be hard to believe, but his article was focused on adoption. Specifically, a private adoption agency that was located in Chicago."

She stared at him, her brow furrowed. "And why would an adoption agency be such a big secret?"

"From what I can tell, he was investigating the agency located here in Chicago because his roommate, Dennis Green, happened to be adopted through them. But that same agency, called New Beginnings, closed down and disappeared fourteen years ago."

"Okay," Shanna said slowly. "But I'm still not clear as to how this helps us."

"Shanna, think about the possibilities. What if Dennis Green was kidnapped for the purposes of being adopted? And what if Skylar was also kidnapped and then adopted out illegally through the same private adoption agency?" He held his breath, hoping he wasn't raising her hopes too high as far as their ability to find Skylar.

EIGHT

Shanna stared at Quinn in disbelief. As much as she wanted to trust his theory, there were too many holes in his logic. "I'm sorry, but that theory really doesn't make sense. Most families want to adopt babies, right? Infants? Or at least kids under a year. I mean, come on, Skylar was five years old."

But even as she voiced the protest, she remembered how everyone thought her sister was younger than she actually was. With her honey-brown hair, big brown eyes and petite frame, Skylar had been adorable.

The old familiar guilt burned low in her belly. Her fault. Skylar's kidnapping had been her fault. And for years she'd feared Skylar had suffered horribly before she'd most likely been killed.

She hoped, prayed that Skylar hadn't suffered.

"I know, I thought the same thing at first," Quinn said, interrupting her dark thoughts. "But from what I read, Brady's theory has some merit. Some families, those who really want a child, will go up a few years in age. Look at how adoptions abroad have expanded over the years. Those kids coming in from foreign countries aren't all infants. And those overseas adoptions take time, along with a significant amount of money. What if you wanted a child now, had the money and didn't want to wait a year or maybe longer to go through the normal process? Maybe these adoption agencies offered a quick turnaround for couples willing to take older kids."

Was he right? The possibility was mind boggling. "Still, I would think that if you were going to kidnap a child to turn around and adopt, why wouldn't you go for younger kids?"

Quinn lifted a shoulder. "Could be that they take what they can get. Parents keep closer eyes on smaller kids. They're either carried or pushed around in a stroller. But those old enough to move under their own power become easier targets."

She shivered because suddenly, Brady's theory made sense. Horrible, chilling sense. She thought about her sister, who might have looked like an easy target. Or the little boy who disappeared from the mall. But there were still a few gaps they needed to understand. "Why did Brady suspect New Beginnings in particular?"

"I think because they were only in existence for a total of five years," Quinn admitted. "But honestly, that's where his theory starts to fall apart. Just because a private adoption agency went out of business didn't mean the owners were breaking the law."

"No, but it's a place to start. I wonder if we should turn this information over to the feds?"

"We probably should, but maybe we need to investigate this link a little further. Right now, we have a lot of assumptions without any concrete proof. We could look at other private adoption agencies to see if there are any common threads."

The thought that other agencies could be doing the exact same thing made her blood congeal in her veins. "There have to be hundreds of private adoption agencies out there."

"I know," Quinn said with a grimace. "But we could try to narrow down our search to those private agencies that aren't in operation anymore. Or those that have only been around for a few years."

She couldn't help feeling the task would be hopeless. What they really needed was some sort of proof that at least one or two of the New Beginnings adoptions were illegal. And going back fourteen years wouldn't make that an easy task. "You really think that your brother was killed because of this article? Because someone found out that he was investigating this particular adoption agency?"

Quinn sighed and shook his head. "I don't know. It sounds far-fetched, doesn't it? But it's a lead, and we can't afford to ignore any potential link. Especially considering your sister disappeared fourteen years ago, as well."

He was right about that, she was forced to admit. The timing of the adoption agency shutting down and her sister's disappearance was almost too much of a coincidence.

Their food arrived just then, interrupting the conversation. Shanna bowed her head to silently give thanks for the food before she began to eat. She sensed Quinn's curious gaze, but when he spoke, he returned to their previous discussion.

"So what information did you come up with?" Quinn asked after digging into his meal.

She took a bite of her burger before answering. "Based on what you just told me, I'm not sure if my information is nearly as helpful. I spoke to Al this morning, and we have a few fingerprint matches. Two kids in particular, Tanya Jacobs and Derek Matthews. They were busted well over a year ago for drug dealing at a state campus in

Milwaukee, Wisconsin. And both of their prints showed up on beer cans from your brother's party."

Quinn's munched a French fry, his expression thoughtful. "Well, that certainly adds an interesting twist."

Privately, she thought the former drug dealers were more likely candidates to have murdered Brady than some stranger from a nonexistent adoption agency. Yet she really liked the adoption-agency theory because she wanted, very badly, to believe Skylar had been adopted into a nice family.

"Yeah, I thought so," she agreed. "Here they are, hanging around a private college in Chicago, their prints found at the scene of your brother's murder. They may or may not be actual students—we can find that out easily enough. But even if they're not officially enrolled, we should get copies of their mug shots and show them around campus."

"Sounds like a good plan," Quinn murmured in agreement as he took another bite of his burger.

They both fell silent as they finished their meal. Shanna kept thinking about the other children who'd been kidnapped about the same time as Skylar. Was it really possible they were all part of some sort of illegal adoption ring? That they were adopted out to other families? Was this what had happened to Skylar?

And to Brady's roommate, Dennis Green?

Quinn noticed Shanna was lost in thought as they finished their lunch. He had a strong feeling his brother had been on to something with his investigation into the New Beginnings adoption agency.

But Shanna's question looped over and over in his mind. Did he really think the adoption article was directly related to Brady's murder?

His cop instincts didn't follow the logic. To think that someone actually linked to the agency, with something to hide, had discovered his brother's investigation and tracked him down to silence him forever was a total and complete stretch.

Logically, it made sense that two students with felony convictions for drug dealing were the more likely candidates for being guilty of a crime of opportunity. Shanna was right about that part; it wasn't as if someone had strategized long and hard about getting Brady alone to kill him. And if someone from the adoption agency was looking for him, it seemed as if they'd go that route, rather than clubbing his brother on the back of the head with a rugby trophy in the early hours of the morning.

Had his brother found out about their drug dealing? Had Brady kicked them out of the party, and they'd come back later for revenge? Or had some other student gone crazy while under the influence of drugs? Any of those scenarios was far more likely.

Shanna was right; they needed to start with the two felons. Finding out if they were actually enrolled in classes or if they just liked hanging out with the college crowd.

"Are you ready?" Quinn asked when the waitress returned with their tab. He took it quickly, before Shanna could try to get all independent on him.

Her smile was a bit lopsided as she nodded. "Yes, I'm ready."

"You look upset," he said with a frown.

"Not at all," she countered quickly. "In fact, I'm glad that we've made so much progress in such a short period of time. I believe God is guiding us, Quinn."

He stared at her for a moment, remembering how she'd said the same thing last evening, before he'd gone to help his mother with Brady's funeral arrangements. And he'd also noticed that she'd bowed her head to pray before eating. He wasn't familiar with the kind of faith she mentioned, so he wasn't sure how to respond.

"Quinn, do you mind if I ask you a personal question?" Shanna's blue eyes were wide and serious.

"Of course not," he responded. After all, they were friends, right? Right.

"Do you believe in God?"

The blunt question took him by surprise. He'd expected some sort of question related to his previous relationships, or why he wasn't married. "Yes," he responded a little too quickly. "Why do you ask?"

"Because I've noticed you get quiet and try to change the subject every time I mention faith or God," she pointed out. "If you didn't believe in God, I could understand that you might be uncomfortable with the subject."

He shrugged, embarrassed that she'd read him so easily. For a moment he remembered the brief prayer he'd said when he found Shanna alive at her house, and the flash of peace. "I was brought up to believe in God, and my parents took me to church services when I was young. But I haven't been to church in years," he said honestly. "So I am a little uncomfortable with the topic, since I can't claim to be in a close relationship with God." And didn't have a clue where to start, even if he wanted to. Which he wasn't at all sure he did.

The smile that lit up her face nearly blinded

him. "That's okay, Quinn. Believing in God is half the battle. He'll forgive you for straying if you want to start fresh. Maybe you need to just give Him a try?"

He stared at her for several long seconds, not sure if he appreciated the opportunity or was afraid of moving forward. Praying inside was one thing; talking out loud was very different. "I'll think about it," he said evasively. And hated himself when the bright light of hope in her eyes dimmed.

"That's all I'll ask," she said, with a smile that looked forced. "I think you'll be surprised if you can find a way to open your heart and your mind."

He wasn't so sure, but he nodded anyway. He signed off on the credit-card receipt and then stood. "Do you still want to go back to Carlyle University to go through student IDs?" he asked.

"Yes. I know there's no guarantee Skylar is a student, but I feel like I need to go through them all anyway, just in case."

He understood her need to be sure. "All right. But on the way, I'm going to stop at the police station to get mug shots of our two suspects, Tanya Jacobs and Derek Matthews."

"I'm interested to see those mug shots, too," she agreed.

For a moment he wondered if it was possible that Tanya Jacobs was actually Shanna's sister,

Skylar. But just as soon as the thought entered his mind, he knew they couldn't be one and the same. Both sets of prints were found at the crime scene, which meant there were two different girls.

Relieved for Shanna's sake, he slung her bag over his shoulder and let her lead the way out of the restaurant. As they went through the lobby to go outside, their fingers brushed and he found himself wishing things could be different. That he had the right to hold her hand.

Friends, he reminded himself. He'd learned the hard way that when it came to women, friendship was all he had to offer.

But it occurred to him as they both climbed into the car that if there ever was a woman he'd want to have a relationship with, she would be exactly like Shanna.

Shanna stayed with Quinn as he inquired at the student-services desk if either Tanya Jacobs or Derek Matthews was enrolled in the university. She wasn't surprised when neither name showed up on the student roster.

"Guess I'll have to show their photos around, see if anyone recognizes them," Quinn muttered, "since the only address on file is the one from Milwaukee."

"Do you want me to help?" Shanna asked, even

though she really wanted to finish up with the student IDs.

Quinn seemed to consider her offer, but then shook his head. "No, thanks. I'll meet you back here in a couple of hours."

Shanna smiled in agreement and then went over to her usual computer workstation. She pulled up the student IDs, trying not to allow her thoughts to dwell on Quinn.

She was glad, very glad, that Quinn believed in God. Now she just needed him to open up to the concept of renewing his faith.

Earlier that morning, when the elevator doors opened and she saw Quinn waiting for her in the lobby, her breath had gotten stuck in her lungs. He'd looked amazing with his black jeans and his long-sleeved white polo shirt. She'd immediately realized that God had brought Quinn into her life for a reason.

Not just to help her find Skylar, but more importantly, so she could help him reconnect with his faith.

When lunch was finished, Quinn had agreed to think about it, and she told herself to be patient. So she sent up a quick prayer, asking God for guidance.

Turning her attention to the task at hand, she flipped through photograph after photograph, trying to see even the slightest resemblance to Skylar's age-progression photo. As she moved slowly through the alphabet of last names, she began to get discouraged. Leaving the *O*'s to start on the last names beginning with the letter *P*, she couldn't help wondering if she was wasting her time going through the photos.

There was no guarantee Skylar looked anything like the age-progression picture. But what else could she do? Now that she was more than halfway through the list, she didn't really want to stop.

Completely lost in the photos, Shanna started when, over an hour later, Quinn came up behind her, putting a light hand on her shoulder. "How's it going?" he asked.

She closed her eyes and willed her heart rate to return to normal. "About the same," she said honestly. "So far no matches anywhere close."

He pulled up a seat beside her. "How many more until you finish the list?"

"Not very many. I'm already up to the *W*'s." She glanced over at him, thinking he seemed tired. "How did it go with the two mug shots?"

"Didn't come up with much. A couple of kids thought the two suspects looked familiar, but couldn't give me any insight as to when or where they saw them last." His tone sounded as dejected as he looked.

More dead ends. Seemed like they took two steps backward for every one step forward.

No, that wasn't fair. She was letting her discouragement get to her. She needed to have faith that God would show them the way.

"You know, if the two of them are involved in anything illegal, like selling drugs, other kids aren't going to be so quick to turn them in," she said.

"Yeah, I thought of that," Quinn said slowly. "But you would still think there are some honest kids who would come forward."

"But honest kids probably haven't interacted with them," she pointed out. "But maybe we're on the wrong track. Maybe we need to start with Brady's roommates. If Brady had spoken to either of the suspects, or argued with them, surely his roommates would have noticed."

"Yeah, I already tried to contact them. The Chicago P.D. has already questioned them and didn't come up with much, at least not according to Hank. And as of today, they were allowed to return to their residence. But when I went over there, no one was around. It would be pretty amazing if they'd already gone back to class."

Very true. But it was possible that going back

to class was exactly what they needed to feel normal. Sometimes getting lost in the normal routine of her life was the only way she could cope with Skylar's kidnapping.

She glanced at her watch, wincing a little when her headache started to return. Time for more ibuprofen. "It's almost four o'clock. If they did go to class, they'll be done soon. Why don't you wait for me to finish here and then we'll both head back over?"

"Your energy level is amazing," Quinn said with a light chuckle. "Okay, you win. We'll work on this together."

She wanted to give her faith credit for her energy level, but decided not to push it. Quinn would find his way, and if God wanted her to intervene, He'd give her a sign.

Finishing the list of female students didn't take long. "Take a look at these five," she suggested, going back to the handful of student images that she'd saved. "Here's the age-progression photo to compare to. What do you think?"

"They're close," Quinn admitted. "But not really a match. Look at the shape of the eyes on this picture." He pointed to the first one. "They slant up, and Skylar's are definitely more round. There are some similarities on these other three, but this last one here is way off. The shape of her face isn't exactly right, either. Skylar's is more heart-shaped, like yours, and hers is oval."

He thought her face was heart-shaped? "Yeah, that was my thought, too, but I wanted to make sure I wasn't being too picky." With a sigh, she shut down the computer. "I guess we know that Skylar isn't likely a student here at the university."

"I'm sorry, Shanna," Quinn murmured.

"It's okay. Every bit of knowledge helps." And she was determined to keep her faith. "If Skylar's not a student, then she must have run into your brother somewhere here on campus."

"I hate to tell you, but Chicago North, an Illinois state campus, is located just six miles from here. The private kids often hang out with the state-school kids."

She grimaced. "I know—I already thought of that. Not just as a place to find Skylar, but as a potential link to our two suspects. Since they were enrolled at a state school in Wisconsin, I thought they might have gone the same route here."

"Let's finish up on this campus first, before we broaden our search too wide," Quinn cautioned.

"All right." But she silently vowed to start looking through the Chicago North student ID listing as soon as possible. There was no reason to suspect Skylar couldn't be a student on that campus. "Are you ready to visit Brady's roommates?"

"Yes." Quinn walked back out with her to his car and drove the couple of blocks to Brady's former residence. It wasn't easy finding a place to park, and they ended up several blocks away.

As they walked up, they ran into Kyle Ryker. "Kyle? Wait up," Quinn called.

The young man glanced at them, and for a moment looked as if he might run. But then he stopped in the middle of the sidewalk, giving them time to catch up. "I already gave my statement to the police," Kyle said defensively.

"I understand how hard this must be for you," Shanna quickly spoke up sympathetically. "And we just have a quick question. Do you remember seeing these two people at the party Saturday night?"

She watched Kyle's eyes as Quinn handed over the photos. There were no telltale signs of recognition, and after a few moments he shook his head. "I'm sorry, but I don't recognize either of them. My girlfriend was over, and I didn't pay a lot of attention to the other kids Brady invited."

"You think Brady invited them?" Quinn asked.

"Either Brady or Dennis. Both of them were passing out flyers to the kids on campus. Mark and I weren't as keen on the thought of having another party. Especially after getting underage-drinking tickets from the last party."

"Thanks. I'd rather you didn't tell your room-mates about these two until we have a chance to show them," Quinn said.

Kyle hunched his shoulders. "Fine with me. I already told the cops my theory about how Brady was playing with fire the way he kept flirting with that new chick all night at the party. Either Anna or one of her friends or even Anna's brother could have smacked him in the head."

She caught her breath and glanced at Quinn, his eyes mirroring her surprise. New chick? "Do you have a name?"

He shrugged. "Phoebe—but don't ask me her last name, 'cause I have no idea."

Phoebe? Shanna's heart raced. Was this the clue they'd been waiting for?

NINE

Quinn eagerly grabbed his wallet from his back pocket and pulled out the list of students they knew for sure were at Brady's party. Quickly, he ran his finger down the neatly typed names.

No Phoebe.

He made a mental note to add her name, now that Kyle had confirmed she was there, as he folded the list and put it back inside his wallet. Then he glanced at the mug shots of the two drug dealers and held up the picture of Tanya Jacobs. "And you're sure this woman isn't Phoebe?"

Kyle studied the picture for a long moment. "Yeah, I'm pretty sure. I mean, they look a little similar I guess, but not a lot. Look, I gotta go." He moved as if to step past them.

"Wait." Shanna stopped him with a hand on his arm. "Can you tell us what Phoebe looks like?"

Kyle rolled his eyes, clearly annoyed with being

detained. "I don't know. She's cute I guess, has long dark hair. But I didn't really pay much attention, 'cause my girl gets jealous, you know?"

"Is she tall? Short? Thin?" Quinn persisted. Surely if she were as cute as Kyle claimed, he could give them a little more information.

"Short and thin, in an athletic sort of way. I swear I don't know anything more. Except that Anna would be mad if she knew how much time Brady spent with her."

"Sounds like you don't like Anna very much," Quinn observed, hearing the distinct note of disdain in Kyle's tone.

"She thinks she's hot stuff, that's all. We don't generally hang with the same crowd. Are we finished now?" His impatience was palpable.

"Yes, thanks. You've been a huge help," Quinn told him. He glanced at Shanna, giving her a nod, so she dropped her hand from Kyle's arm.

"Yes, thanks, Kyle," she added sincerely. "Take care, okay?"

"Sure," he said half over his shoulder, picking up his pace until he was jogging to get away from them.

"What do you think?" Shanna asked when Kyle was out of earshot. "Is it possible your brother was killed because of some sort of love triangle?"

"I don't know what to think," he muttered. "Except that we have more suspects than we know what to do with."

"Usually it's the opposite problem, isn't it?" Shanna murmured.

"True enough. Phoebe wasn't on the list of party attendees, so at least we have another name to add. And there is a slight possibility that Phoebe is Tanya Jacobs. I hope we don't have to go through the entire list of all female students enrolled here at Carlyle again, looking for her."

"At least we can cross-reference her first name," Shanna pointed out. "And it's original enough that there probably won't be more than one."

She was right about that. "So do we head back to the chancellor's office before they close? Or continue looking for Dennis Green and Mark Pickard?"

"We can call first thing in the morning to find out about Phoebe. Let's just keep looking for Brady's roommates."

Quinn was glad Shanna's thoughts were in complete alignment with his. "Let's go then, see if the other two guys are home yet."

As Shanna fell into step beside him, he wondered how to convince her to return to the hotel later tonight. The threat of danger was diluted in the bright daylight, but it was less than twenty-four hours ago that he'd found her lying in her house, bleeding from a head injury.

No way did he want to risk anything like that again. Yet he wasn't sure she'd appreciate him sticking his nose into her business.

Unfortunately, they didn't have any more luck with Dennis or Mark. The guys didn't recognize the two mug shots as kids who'd attended the party, and of course they also didn't know the infamous Phoebe's last name, either.

"If you remember anything or run into this Phoebe, will you please give me a call?" Quinn asked, handing over copies of his business cards.

The boys took the cards with obvious reluctance. "Yeah, sure," Dennis said. Mark put his card in his pocket without even looking at it.

He knew he shouldn't be frustrated with the lack of information and cooperation from Brady's roommates, but he was.

"Not sure I believe they'll ever call," Shanna murmured as they turned and walked away.

Quinn agreed with her assessment. "Yeah, I guess talking to the cops isn't high on their list of fun things to do."

Shanna scowled. "You'd think they'd want to help find Brady's killer."

The same thought had occurred to him, as well. Maybe they'd given up too hastily on considering the roommates as potential suspects. Just because a group of guys lived together didn't make them best friends. Hadn't Kyle confirmed they didn't hang out with the same group of kids? Maybe as long as each guy held up their end of the financial side of things, like rent and utilities and food, nothing else mattered?

"Come on," he said, taking Shanna's arm. "Let's grab a quick bite to eat and then head over to the library."

"The library?" she echoed in surprise. "Why? I can't imagine that the kids who hang out in a library will have much interaction with drug dealers."

"No, probably not. And that's assuming that these two are still in the drug-dealing business. Earlier, when I called Anna to set up a meeting, she was in class. But she told me she'd be studying at the library tonight. Let's see if she recognizes either of these suspects as kids who've been hanging around Brady."

And maybe, just maybe, Brady's former girlfriend would know where to find the mysterious Phoebe.

Shanna ordered a salad, still full from the burger she'd had for lunch. She once again said a quick prayer before eating, and this time, instead of staring at her, Quinn bowed his head, respectfully waiting for her to finish before he opened his fast-food meal. He didn't say anything, though, just dug into his food with gusto. She watched in amazement, impressed by his voracious appetite. She wasn't used to how much food a man could put away, but then again, her experience with men was rather limited.

Garrett probably wasn't the best yardstick to measure other men by, since he'd gotten very frustrated with her early on in their relationship. She'd tried, but just hadn't been able to take their relationship to the next level. She'd cared about him as a friend, but nothing more. She'd thought maybe her feelings would change over time, but Garrett hadn't been interested in waiting around.

For some reason, she didn't get the impression Quinn would give up as easily. Not that she was looking to turn their friendship into something more.

"Should I offer a quarter for your thoughts?" Quinn asked, breaking the silence. "You seem pretty intent."

She almost choked on a piece of chicken from her salad. No way was she going to mention that she was thinking about Quinn. "Actually, I'm wondering about Phoebe, the girl your brother was flirting with at the party. Do you think it's possible she might be Skylar?"

"I actually doubt it, only because of Brady's article on adoption."

She frowned. "What do you mean?"

"Well, he mentions Dennis Green's adoption. Don't you think he might have mentioned Phoebe if he knew she was adopted too?"

"Good point," she said with a sigh. "I suppose it's possible Phoebe is adopted but doesn't know because her parents never told her?"

"I doubt her parents could get away with that, considering they wouldn't have any baby pictures of her—any pictures at all until she was five, right?"

"You're right. Again." She'd been so hopeful that they'd finally had a lead on Skylar. Best for her to remember there were roughly fifty people at the party, and Skylar could have been any one of them.

"Are you done?" Quinn asked when he'd finished his fish sandwich and fries.

She stared at her salad, surprised that she'd managed to eat most of it. "Yes, I'm finished."

As they left the fast-food restaurant, she noticed the sun was low on the horizon. She loved fall, with the brightly colored changing leaves and the cooler temperatures, but she wasn't thrilled with having shorter days. Quinn headed toward the last row where his SUV was parked, but she hung back. "Quinn, the library is only a couple of blocks away. Why don't we walk?" she suggested. "Maybe we'll pass some kids who fit the description of our two suspects."

"Good thinking," he agreed.

There were a fair amount of students milling around the campus, even at six o'clock in the evening. By mutual agreement, they kept their pace slow, giving them plenty of time to scan the faces of the students. When Quinn's fingers brushed hers, she took his hand, and then blushed when he glanced at her in surprise. "We might get further with questioning these kids if we don't act like cops," she said, by way of explanation.

His slow grin, and the way his hand gently and firmly cupped hers, made her chest tighten with awareness. Flustered, she averted her gaze and tried to focus on finding their suspects, which wasn't easy with Quinn holding her hand.

Poor judgment on her part, to pretend they were a couple as a way to blend into the crowd. She liked being with him a little too much.

"Hey, look over there," Quinn said in a low voice, gesturing to the right with their joined hands. "See that small group of kids next to the commons? Do they seem to be acting suspicious to you?"

She stared, trying to figure out what had caught his attention. "Not really, why? Am I missing something?"

"Could be nothing, or it could be some sort of drug deal going down," Quinn muttered. "Hard to tell from here."

She glanced at him, wondering what it must be like to see possible criminal activity on every corner. Obviously, he patrolled this area a lot in his job, on the lookout for anything suspicious. At least when she was called in to gather evidence, the crime had already been committed. But as a cop, Quinn's duty was to try to prevent crimes from happening, if possible.

She slowed to a stop, letting go of his hand to kneel down, pretending to tie her shoe. "Do you want to go over there?" she asked. "I can wait here."

"No, they're already breaking up and heading in different directions," he said. "And none of them look familiar. Maybe it really was nothing."

"Do you want to follow one of them?" she asked, not sure what he would normally do if he were alone.

"No, let's head over to the library. I think our time is better spent questioning Anna Belfast."

She hoped so. When she stood, he once again took possession of her hand.

They reached the library a few minutes later, and she glanced around curiously. There were more students in the library than she'd expected, and half of them were sitting on overstuffed chairs, working on laptops. The rest seemed to be studying from textbooks.

"Did Anna give you a hint as to where she usually studies?" she asked.

"No. But maybe we should split up, since we can cover more ground that way," Quinn said. "I'll make color copies of the mug shots for you."

"Except I don't know what Anna looks like," she protested.

"That's right. I forgot." Quinn headed over to two copy machines along the wall. He made the color copies and handed one set to her. "Okay, let's find Anna first, and then we can split up to question the rest of the kids."

She definitely liked that plan better. She followed his lead, wandering through the expansive library.

"Over there," Quinn said. "See the blonde sitting in the orange chair? That's Maggie, Anna's roommate. But I don't see any sign of Anna."

Before she could respond, Quinn walked over to the spot where Maggie sat.

"Hi, Maggie," he greeted her, smiling as if they were long-lost friends. "How are you?"

She looked up at him blankly, but then recognition slowly dawned. "Well, if it isn't Officer Murphy," she responded in a cool tone. "What brings you here?"

"I'm looking for your roommate, Anna. Is she around?"

Maggie shrugged and glanced around rather pointedly. "She's not here that I can see. What makes you think I know where she is?"

"Because Anna told me you'd both be here studying for an exam. Didn't she mention that to you?"

Maggie frowned. "No, she didn't."

Shanna stepped forward, hoping maybe she could connect with Maggie on a woman-to-woman level. "Hi, Maggie. My name is Shanna Dawson. Can you tell me if you recognize either of these two people?" She showed Maggie the mug shots of Tanya Jacobs and Derek Matthews.

Maggie made a face and shook her head. "I don't know anyone who spent time in jail."

It was unfortunate they didn't have other photos of the two kids, since there was no disguising a mug shot. "They were arrested a year ago, and they're out now. Isn't it possible you've maybe seen them around campus? I mean, you wouldn't know they did jail time, right?"

Maggie's eyes narrowed, and she looked again at the two mug shots. "They still don't look familiar, although there are a lot of kids here. I only just transferred here this fall, so I don't know a lot of the students yet."

"I understand," Shanna said sympathetically. "But maybe if you do see them, you'll give us a call?" She handed over one of Quinn's business cards.

"I suppose I could do that." At least Maggie looked at the card, then back up at Quinn, before tucking it inside her purse.

"So you and Anna didn't come to the library together?" Quinn asked, turning the subject back to Brady's former girlfriend.

"No." When Quinn just stood there staring at her, she squirmed in her seat. "She did say she might meet me here later," Maggie finally admitted.

"We'll hang around for a while and wait for her, then," Quinn said.

"By the way, Maggie, do you know Phoebe?" Shanna asked before Quinn could turn away.

There was a flicker of something, recognition

maybe, in her eyes, but she shook her head. "No, I don't."

"But you've heard her name, right?" Shanna persisted.

"Yeah, maybe. It sounds familiar, but I don't know her," Maggie insisted. "And if you don't mind, I really need to study. I can't afford to flunk this exam."

She glanced at Quinn, trying to read the expression in his eyes. Did he think Maggie was lying? Or telling the truth?

"Sure thing," Quinn said easily. "Good luck with your studying."

Shanna followed his lead, moving away from Maggie until they were out of earshot. "What do you think?" she whispered. "Is she being honest with us?"

"I think so," Quinn murmured. "Considering Kyle's comments earlier, could be that Anna heard about Brady's flirting with Phoebe through the grapevine. It's not a stretch to think she shared the news with her roommate."

Quinn's logic made sense. "So now what? Do we hang out here waiting for Anna?"

"Let's split up for a bit," he suggested. "And see if anyone else recognizes either the photos of our two suspects or the name Phoebe."

"All right, let's meet back here in thirty minutes."

Shanna headed to the opposite end of the library from Quinn, showing several students the photographs. But no one seemed to recognize the two former drug dealers as anyone they'd seen around campus. And even worse, no one admitted to knowing anyone by the name of Phoebe.

She tried not to get discouraged, knowing from firsthand experience that key information was often discovered when you least expected it. Much of the evidence she collected in her role as a crime-scene investigator was from sheer determination and tedious attention to detail.

But she'd really been hoping for a break, especially in uncovering the identity of the mysterious Phoebe. Even though she agreed with Quinn's theory that Phoebe was likely not Skylar, she couldn't help feeling as if finding the girl would help crack their case wide open.

But then again, finding Phoebe could be nothing more than another dead end.

She returned to the center of the library, where she'd promised to meet Quinn. Maggie was still sprawled in her orange overstuffed chair, studying. She waited a few minutes to see if Maggie noticed her standing there, but she didn't.

Quinn walked up a minute later. "Any luck?"

"No."

"Me, neither." He glanced at his watch, then

over to where Maggie was studying, a frown furrowing his brow. "Anna should be here by now."

"Maybe you scared her off?" she suggested.

Quinn sent a sideways glance in her direction. "She doesn't have a reason to be afraid, unless she happens to be guilty of something."

"Some people just don't like talking to the police," she said. "And as Brady's girlfriend, she must know she's a potential suspect."

"Yeah, maybe." Quinn seemed uncharacteristically indecisive. "Should we wait here? Or head over to her dorm room?"

"Hey, look." She gave his arm a tug. "Maggie's packing up her books."

Quinn's scowl deepened, and he immediately headed over to the girl. "Finished studying already?" he asked.

"You're making me nervous, standing there staring at me," the girl said defiantly. "So I'm leaving."

"Have you heard from Anna?" Quinn persisted, blocking Maggie's path. "Or maybe I have that backwards. Maybe you called Anna, telling her not to come?"

Maggie's face went pale. "I didn't call her, and I didn't hear from her, either. Check my phone," she said, thrusting it at him.

"You could have erased the messages," he said after giving the screen a cursory look.

"I don't even know how to delete the memory," Maggie argued. "But have it your way." She waited for Quinn to step aside before heading out of the library.

Shanna wasn't surprised when Quinn followed the girl outside. Maggie had to have known they were behind her, but she didn't glance back even once.

"Guess we're going to Anna's dorm room, huh?" Shanna asked in a low tone.

"Might as well, since I don't have any other bright ideas as to where she might be."

Just then, Maggie, who was a few yards ahead of them, lifted up a hand and waved frantically. "Anna!" she called. "Over here!"

A dark haired girl turned to look, but must have seen Quinn because she abruptly spun away, taking off at a run.

"What is she doing?" Quinn muttered, breaking into a jog to catch up with her. Shanna sprinted after Quinn, while Maggie stood there, staring in shock.

The section of the sidewalk they were on disappeared, due to some sort of construction, so they went out into the road. As they came up to an intersection, bright headlights blinded her from a car heading toward them.

She winced and slowed down, the lights intensifying the dull ache in her head. She hoped the car would hurry up and pass her by, but instead, the car picked up speed.

Realization dawned just a little too late.

"Look out!" Quinn shouted.

TEN

Quinn grabbed Shanna's arm, wrenching her out of harm's way, the momentum bringing her solidly up against him. The last-minute motion saved their lives, as the car missed them by inches, hitting several of the orange construction barrels and sending them flying through the air.

He clutched her close, his heart lodged in his throat and a loud roaring echoing in his ears. The way her arms were clamped around his waist betrayed how frightened she was. Not that he could blame her.

Close. That was way too close.

Thank You for keeping her safe, Lord.

The whispered prayer came instantly to his mind, and he couldn't help but wonder if Shanna was right about having faith. Maybe he could learn something from her.

"Are you okay?" He managed to find his voice after a long minute. The taillights of the car had already disappeared down the street, and he couldn't help feeling frustrated that he hadn't been able to get the tag number.

No way did he think this was some sort of accident. Not after the way Shanna had been attacked in her home the evening before.

"Yes." The sound of her voice was muffled by her face buried against his chest. He ran a reassuring hand down her back, thinking he could hold her like this forever.

But, of course, Shanna was too strong, too independent to lean against him for long. All too soon, she loosened her grip, lifted her head and took a step back. He reluctantly released her, although he kept a steadying hand on her arm, unable to break all physical contact with her.

"That guy shouldn't be allowed to keep his license," she said grimly, pushing her tangled dark hair away from her face.

"Shanna, it wasn't an accident. He headed straight for you," he said, his tone coming out harsher than he'd intended.

She glanced up at him in surprise. "Are you sure? Because for a moment I thought he was heading toward Maggie."

"Maggie?" Quinn spun around, sweeping the area with his gaze, searching for Anna's roommate. Then he saw her about ten yards away, sitting next to a grassy embankment beside two orange barrels lying on their sides. Quickly, he headed over. "Maggie? Are you all right?"

Maggie lifted her head, and the sight of her tear-streaked cheeks hit him hard. He knelt beside her, searching for signs of injury.

"I'm fine," she said, brushing her fingertips over her damp cheeks. "Just scared."

"I don't blame you for being scared," Quinn murmured. "You're sure you don't hurt anywhere?"

"I'm sure. I jumped out of the way," Maggie admitted. "But I didn't think he was trying to hit me. From what I saw, he was heading straight for her," she said, waving a hand at Shanna who'd come over to stand beside him.

"I'm so glad you weren't hurt," Quinn said.

"Me, too," Shanna agreed. "Maggie, did you recognize the car at all?"

"I couldn't even see the car with the bright headlights blinding me," she admitted.

"I know. I think he had the high-beam lights on," Shanna said. "I couldn't see what sort of car he was driving, either."

"I'm pretty sure it was a dark green Honda Accord," Quinn said. "But I only caught a glimpse once I realized the idiot driver was trying to hit you." Replaying the sequence of events in his mind, he couldn't say for sure which woman was the primary target, since Maggie had been just a short distance from Shanna. It was pure luck that he'd noticed and had time to yank Shanna out of harm's way.

He was ashamed to admit he hadn't even thought of Maggie.

But no matter what Shanna's or Maggie's impressions were, he firmly believed this was the work of Shanna's stalker. The guy must be following her, since their decision to go to the library had been made on the spur of the moment.

"But I don't understand. Why would he try to hit one of us?" Maggie asked.

"I feel like I should apologize to you, Maggie, because I was probably the real target," Shanna said. "Some creepy guy has been stalking me."

Quinn was surprised at how Shanna took the blame. Obviously, after thinking about it, she logically knew she must be the target. But what about her impression that he'd aimed for Maggie? Unless in the darkness, he'd momentarily mistook Maggie for Shanna?

"You have a stalker?" Maggie echoed in horror. "That's awful. So he really was trying to hit you?"

"I'm afraid so," Shanna said. "I'm so sorry."

"That's okay," the young student murmured.

And Quinn sensed Maggie was somehow relieved by the news.

"Maggie, why did Anna run away?" he asked, bringing the conversation back to the events prior to the attempted hit-and-run.

Maggie's expression turned guarded. "I don't know what you mean."

Quinn's patience thinned. "Stop it," he said with a touch of annoyance. "Be honest. You waved at her, and the minute Anna saw me, she took off running. Tell me what's going on. Is she afraid to talk to me for some reason?"

Maggie's shoulders slumped, and Quinn sensed he finally got through to her when she reluctantly nodded. "Yes. She is afraid to talk to you. She's afraid you're going to try to prove she hurt Brady. And frankly, I'm tired of being dragged into Anna's problems."

Quinn couldn't help the surge of satisfaction. "She never planned on coming to the library tonight, did she?"

"No, she didn't," Maggie admitted. "I'm sorry."

"That's okay," Shanna said soothingly. "It's not your fault."

Quinn didn't necessarily agree since Maggie willingly tried to protect her roommate, but he kept quiet, sensing Shanna had a better chance of getting through to Maggie than he did.

"You don't have to keep protecting Anna," Shanna continued. "Loyalty is one thing, but breaking the law is something completely different."

"I wasn't lying about Anna being in the dorm the night of Brady's party," she said earnestly. "Anna isn't perfect, but she wouldn't murder anyone. Especially not Brady. She loved him."

Quinn wasn't sure he believed that, either. "I heard she got mad at Brady and that she has quite the temper."

"She might get mad easily, but I've never seen her hit or be violent with anyone, ever," Maggie protested.

There was always a first, but he didn't mention that. For some reason, he couldn't help feeling Anna held a key to the mystery surrounding Brady's death. "Tell me the truth, Maggie. Anna was mad at Brady, wasn't she?"

"She was mad he'd planned a party on the night of her last performance," Maggie admitted. "But that's all. She was annoyed more than anything, certainly not angry enough to hit him in the head."

"Are you sure she wasn't upset with Brady because he was flirting with other girls?" Shanna persisted.

At first, Maggie shook her head, but then she

shrugged. "That might have been part of the issue with the party," she allowed. "I mean, he knew Anna couldn't come to the party due to the performance, right? So maybe she did wonder if there was another girl. Anna didn't confide in me that Brady might be cheating on her, though."

Cheating with the infamous Phoebe? Quinn wished he knew for certain. "Okay, thanks for your help," Quinn said. He stood and held out a hand to help Maggie up. "Now, how about we walk you back to your dorm room?"

"Sure," Maggie murmured, taking Quinn's hand and allowing him to assist her. "But I have to tell you, I doubt you'll find Anna there."

"We just want to make sure you get home safe," Shanna said quickly.

They walked across campus, heading for Dorchester Hall, where Maggie and Anna lived. Once inside, they took the elevator to the seventh floor.

"Room 724?" he asked, as they stepped out of the elevator.

"Yes, this way," Maggie said, taking the first corridor to the right.

He and Shanna waited patiently as Maggie pulled out her key and unlocked the door. She pushed it open and then waved a hand. "See? Told you she wouldn't be here."

Quinn poked his head inside the room, verifying that it was indeed empty. Both girls had their beds raised up off the floor on stilts to give them more space to sit underneath. Clothes jammed the closets, spilling out onto the floors, so there was no way to hide in there, either. The dorm room was messy but definitely empty.

"Thanks Maggie," he said, moving back outside. "I'm sure it won't do any good, but tell Anna I'd still like to talk to her, okay?"

"Try to reassure her that we don't believe she hurt Brady," Shanna interjected. "But we do want to know more about Brady's friends. Because someone at his party struck him in the back of the head and killed him. Anything more she can tell us might help."

"I'll tell her," Maggie said. "I'm not sure it will help any, but I'll try to convince her to cooperate."

"That's all we can ask," Shanna said. "Take care, Maggie."

"Bye," Maggie said, before closing the dorm-room door.

Quinn let Shanna lead the way back to the elevators. It was too late to go looking for Anna any more tonight. Besides, he had an almost desperate urge to get Shanna somewhere safe.

"That was an interesting night," she said as they rode the elevator down to the lobby.

Interesting wasn't the word he would have used. But he noticed she usually downplayed the danger she was in.

"Shanna, will you do me a favor?"

She hesitated for a moment. "Maybe. What kind of favor?"

"After everything that's happened, will you please let me take you back to the hotel tonight?"

For a moment, she grimaced as if she might argue, but then she slowly nodded. "All right, Quinn. I'll go back to the hotel for another night."

He didn't bother to hide his relief. "Thanks, Shanna." He was glad she didn't try to fight him on this issue.

And as they walked through the Dorchester Hall lobby and headed outside, he decided that this time, nothing was going to prevent him from staying in a room at the hotel with her.

Nothing.

Shanna couldn't believe it when Quinn asked for two hotel rooms side by side. She didn't have her same room, since she'd checked out earlier that morning. "There's no need," she tried to tell him, but he clearly wasn't listening.

"Thanks," he said to the clerk behind the desk, as he took both room keys and then slung her duffel bag over his shoulder.

"You don't even have any luggage," she tried pointing out, catching up with him as he strode toward the elevators. "Quinn, be reasonable. You made sure no one followed us. I'm perfectly safe here."

"I'm not leaving you," he said flatly.

His protectiveness was sweet, but she couldn't help feeling guilty. She knew she was keeping him from investigating his brother's death. And yet he'd asked her to come here for the night, as a favor to him.

There had to be something she could do to help him.

He paused outside the first room, handing her the key and waiting while she unlocked the door. "Thanks, Quinn," she said, when he finally handed over her bag. She swung the bag inside the room, setting it on the floor with a thud.

"You're welcome," he said, bracing his arm on the door frame and staring down at her for a long moment.

His gaze was mesmerizing, making it impossible for her to look away. She sensed he wanted to say something, but then he surprised her by bending to press his mouth warmly against hers.

Her lips clung to his, and she reveled in the sensation, remembering those moments when he'd held her close in his arms. But the kiss was over too quickly, as he broke away and took a step back. "Remember, I'm right next door if you need anything," he said gruffly.

Unable to speak, she could only nod and watch, bemused as he took the few steps to get to the next door down.

"Good night, Quinn," she finally managed, after he unlocked his door and waited rather obviously for her to go inside.

"Good night, Shanna." Only after she shut and locked her door did she hear the click of his door closing.

And she couldn't help admitting how incredibly safe she felt, knowing Quinn was right on the other side of the wall.

The next morning her phone rang, waking her from a sound sleep. "Yes?" she answered groggily.

"Shanna? Would you like to meet me for breakfast?" Quinn asked.

She blinked away her fatigue, thinking he sounded far too cheerful considering the early hour. "Uh, sure. Could you give me about a half hour to get ready?"

"No problem," he assured her. "Meet me downstairs in the restaurant, okay?"

"Sure." She hung up the phone and pushed her

hair out of her eyes, yawning widely. She'd struggled to fall asleep last night, her mind dwelling on Quinn's kiss. Reliving the moment. Wondering why he'd kissed her. Wondering if he'd kiss her again.

Pathetic. She needed to stop thinking about Quinn and the feelings she was beginning to have for him and keep focused on trying to find Skylar.

It took her a little longer to get ready, making her a few minutes late when she finally arrived in the restaurant. Quinn didn't seem impatient; he was just sipping a mug of coffee and reading the paper.

"Sorry," she murmured, sliding into the seat across from him in the booth.

"No problem." He folded the paper and tucked it away. "I'm sorry, Shanna, but I'll need to drop you off somewhere this morning. I have a few errands I have to run for my mother."

"Oh, sure. Of course." Flustered, she glanced at the menu, but then brought her gaze back up to meet his. "We can skip breakfast if you need to get going."

"No, please. Order whatever you'd like."

Quinn seemed anxious to leave, so she decided to order a simple bowl of oatmeal. Quinn surprised her by choosing the same thing.

"Is everything okay?" she asked after the waitress left.

"Yes, it's fine," he answered. "But my brother's body is being released today and my mother needs some emotional support."

"I understand." And she truly did. After the way Skylar's kidnapping ripped her family apart, she knew only too well the impact of a terrible tragedy. Thinking of Quinn's mother made her wonder if she should try, once again, to talk to her father. After all, he couldn't keep ignoring her forever. Could he?

Maybe once they found Skylar, he'd find it in his heart to forgive her.

When their food arrived, Shanna bowed her head and prayed. "Thank You, heavenly Father, for this food we are about to eat. And guide us on Your chosen path while keeping us safe in Your care. Amen."

"Amen," Quinn echoed.

Startled, she opened her eyes and looked at him. She hadn't even realized she'd spoken out loud until he'd responded. "Sounds as if maybe you've found your faith after all," she said.

Quinn slowly nodded. "I haven't prayed in a long time," he admitted. "But I've found myself thanking God for saving you, both last night when you narrowly missed being hit by that car, and the night before when I found you lying unconscious in your doorway. Praying has given me peace. And I can't help but think God really is watching over you."

She was touched by his admission. "God is watching over all of us, not just me. He's watching over you, too, Quinn. He's always with us, even if we're not always paying attention."

A ghost of a smile played along his features. "I hope so."

"I know so," she argued lightly. "Trust me."

"I do trust you, Shanna," he said seriously. "Very much."

The waitress interrupted then, asking how their food was and they assured her the oatmeal was fine.

"Where would you like me to drop you off?" Quinn asked, as he prepared to pay the bill.

"My house."

He narrowed his gaze. "Shanna, I'm not so sure that's a good idea."

"I need a change of clothes and I need my car. There's no reason you have to drive me around everywhere I go."

"There is a reason for me to drive you around." Quinn's expression turned stubborn. "For one thing, we know this guy has followed you, so he knows what car you're driving. And a red Camry will be easy to find and follow. For another, I think it's better if we stay together, so he has less of a chance to find you alone."

She knew attempting to get her car was a long shot, but she'd wanted to give it a try. Quinn was going out of his way to be nice, but she still couldn't help feeling guilty. "Surely you have better things to do than cart me around."

"Nope."

She sighed and gave up, realizing that if she kept arguing he'd be delayed even more. "Okay, then for now drop me off at Carlyle's admissions office. Later, you're going to have to take me home so I can get a change of clothes."

"What are you going to do at the university?" he asked as they left the restaurant and headed out to his SUV.

She waited until he'd stored her overnight bag in the back and climbed into the driver's seat. "I'm going to search for Phoebe."

"Okay." Quinn started the engine and backed out of the parking space. "Promise me you'll keep me posted on whatever you find."

"I will."

The ride from the hotel to the university didn't take long. When she reached for her bag, Quinn's brows rose in surprise but he didn't say anything other than promising to call her once he was finished before he drove away.

Shanna returned to the computer station she'd begun to consider her own, and began searching for students with the first name Phoebe.

Nothing.

She stared and tried again, using Phoebe as the last name. Still nothing. She unzipped her bag and dug out the articles related to the other children who'd gone missing around the same time as Skylar.

Her gaze settled on the Kenny Larson story, the four-year-old who'd been kidnapped from the shopping mall. To refresh her memory, she read through the article and then turned back to the computer.

After finding the website dedicated to missing children, she pulled up Kenny Larson's page, just to make sure nothing had changed and that he hadn't been found.

Unfortunately, Kenny Larson was still listed as missing. So she clicked on the age-progression photo. For several long minutes, she stared at the picture, trying to figure out why the face looked familiar.

Then suddenly she knew. Dennis Green. Her heart leaped as she quickly pulled up his university ID. Seeing the two photos side by side, there was no mistake. They were one and the same.

Dennis Green was really Kenny Larson.

ELEVEN

Numb with shock, Shanna stared at the two matching photographs. Looking closer, she could see they weren't exactly the same—age progression could only do so much—but the similarities were uncanny. In her mind, there was no denying Dennis Green and Kenny Larson were one and the same.

The evidence proving that Brady had been onto something when he'd begun his investigation into the New Beginnings Adoption Agency was chilling.

Why hadn't she considered sooner the possibility that Dennis Green was one of these missing kids? Keeping her gaze locked on the photos as if they might disappear, she reached with trembling fingers for her phone.

Tearing her gaze away just long enough to dial Quinn's number, she held her breath as she waited for him to answer.

Sharp disappointment stabbed deep when the call went straight through to voice mail. She took a breath and let it out slowly. "Quinn? It's Shanna. Call me when you have a minute. It's important."

She hung up without saying anything more.

Now what? Staring at the proof before her that at least one missing child had ended up adopted by another family, she wasn't sure how to proceed from here.

Except that they absolutely had to get the FBI involved. Certainly, the federal government had far better resources to begin investigating deeper into the New Beginnings Adoption Agency. And Kenny Larson's family deserved to know their long-lost son was alive and safe.

They'd gone off on the wrong track, thinking that Brady's death was related to some sort of presumed love triangle. It could be that the mysterious Phoebe was nothing more than some girl who'd flirted harmlessly with Brady during a party.

But then, why had Anna acted so strangely? In her experience, innocent people didn't shy away from the police.

She glanced at her phone impatiently, willing Quinn to return her call. Because now that they had this link, she desperately wanted to see Brady's notes related to the adoption agency.

Kenny Larson had been found, but Skylar, along with dozens of other children, was still missing.

For a moment, she considered calling her mother with the news. Surely, once the FBI became involved, they'd be able to track down all the adoptees from New Beginnings and solve many of the crimes. They'd find Skylar now, even without knowing her fingerprints were at the crime scene.

But tracking down the rest of the missing children through the link of the New Beginnings Adoption Agency didn't solve the mystery of who killed Brady.

The shrill ringing of her phone startled her, and she reached for it eagerly. "Quinn?"

"I just picked up your message," he said. "What's going on? Are you all right?"

"I'm fine," she hastened to assure him. "Can you get here soon? I want to show you what I found."

"You found Phoebe?" he said, his voice rising with excitement.

"No. But I'm looking at proof that Brady's roommate, Dennis Green, is Kenny Larson."

"Kenny Larson?" Quinn echoed in a puzzled tone.

"Remember the four-year-old who was taken from the shopping mall about nine months before

Skylar's disappearance?" she asked. "They're the same person, Quinn. I think your brother was on to something with his investigation into the New Beginnings Adoption Agency."

"Stay right where you are. I'll be there in less than fifteen minutes."

Quinn snapped his phone shut and glanced over at his mother. She looked as if she'd aged ten years in the four days since Brady's death. His heart ached for her, yet at the same time, he couldn't help wondering if his mother's grief would be more tolerable if she had the same level of faith Shanna did.

"There's been a break in the case, Mom. I have to leave."

Fevered hope flared in his mother's tired, red-rimmed eyes. "A break in the case? You've found the person who killed my son?"

"We've found another piece of the puzzle," Quinn corrected, unwilling to raise his mother's hopes too high. He glanced at his watch to verify the time. Her mother's husband, James, would be home in less than an hour. "If you think you'll be all right here until James gets home, I'd like to go and see where this clue leads us."

She blew her nose and sniffled loudly. "All right, but call me as soon as you know *anything.*"

He wasn't going to call her unless he had irrefutable proof, but he nodded and leaned over to give her a kiss on the cheek. "Bye, Mom. I love you."

"Bye, Quinn." There was a distinct pause before she added, "I love you, too."

Hoping he'd made a little headway in the troubled relationship with his mother, Quinn jogged out to his car, feeling more elated than he had in a long time.

It occurred to him as he drove quickly back to the university that one way his life seemed to be taking a positive turn was because of Shanna.

And maybe more so, as a direct result of renewing his faith and renewing his relationship with God.

Thank You, Lord. Please keep my mother, her husband and Ivy safe in Your care.

The silent prayer made him feel much better. He parked outside the university admissions office and hurried inside to find Shanna. His heart thudded loudly in his chest when he saw her rise up to greet him.

Acting instinctively, he embraced her in a warm hug. Time seemed to freeze momentarily as her arms tightened around his waist, hugging him back.

He could have held her like this forever, but

after a long moment he forced himself to release her and step back. "Show me what you found," he murmured huskily.

"Look at this," she said enthusiastically as she resumed her seat in front of the computer screen. He sank into a chair beside her as she refreshed the image.

Two side-by-side photos took up the entire computer screen, and he immediately agreed with her assessment. The age-progression image of Kenny Larson was remarkably similar to the college ID photo of Dennis Green.

"This is huge, Shanna," he said, awed by her discovery. "We have to take this to the authorities. The police first and then probably the FBI."

"I know. I didn't want to call Detective Hank Nelson without showing you first."

He glanced at Shanna, surprised by her apparent loyalty. When had the two of them become a closely knit team?

Since the first night when they'd had coffee together and he'd followed Shanna home, he slowly realized. Somehow, after that first encounter, they'd worked together and managed to accomplish amazing results.

The proof of those results was staring them in the face.

"Thanks," he murmured. "I appreciate you including me in this. I think we should make a copy of this evidence, both on a flash drive and on paper, and take them down to the Chicago P.D."

"Good idea, except I don't have a flash drive."

"I do." He pulled out the one he'd used to download all of the files from Brady's computer. He quickly inserted it into the university computer and copied the photos. Then he printed them on a color printer. The paper wasn't photo paper, but the image was good enough, in his estimation, to convince Hank to contact the feds.

"All right, let's go," he said as he disconnected the flash drive.

Shanna gathered her files and newspaper articles together and stuffed them back into her duffel bag.

He held the door for Shanna. "I'm parked over there," he said, gesturing with one hand to where his SUV waited two blocks down the street.

"I see it," Shanna said, heading in that direction.

He stayed behind her, his gaze sweeping the area, looking for any sign of her stalker. Granted, it was the middle of the day, rather than the dark of night, but he couldn't help thinking that this guy was still following her.

Last night, they'd been walking along the road when he'd come after her in his car. It could have been a coincidence that he saw her along the road and drove straight for her on impulse, but then again, the stalker could just as easily have tagged his car the night he'd found Shanna unconscious and had been following his car ever since.

Either way, he wasn't taking any chances.

She tucked her overnight case in the backseat before opening the passenger door. He swept his gaze across the area once again, and paused when he noticed a familiar couple standing on the street corner near the commons. The two drug-dealing felons. On the exact same corner, where he'd noticed the small group of kids gathered last night.

"Shanna, get in the car and lock the doors. I'll be right back." He spun on his heel and headed over to where the group of kids appeared to be in deep conversation.

When he heard the door of his SUV close, he relaxed, knowing Shanna was safe. Quickening his pace, he kept his gaze locked on the kids.

His instincts were on high alert. He'd bet his last paycheck that a drug deal was going down right there in front of the commons, in broad daylight.

He was maybe ten yards away when the familiar face of their suspect, Derek Matthews, lifted and looked directly at Quinn. Their eyes locked and, suddenly, Derek broke away from the group, taking off on foot in the opposite direction.

"Stop! Police!" Quinn shouted, sprinting after Derek. Luckily, the area around the commons was crowded with students, slowing Derek's progress.

"Stop! Police!" Quinn yelled again, hoping, praying one of the kids would help out. And suddenly, one of the students did exactly that—stuck out a leg and tripped Derek so that he stumbled and fell, falling face-first onto the concrete.

Quinn picked up his pace, catching up with Derek before he could jump back up to his feet and take off again. "Don't try it," Quinn advised. He knelt on Derek's back, forcing him to stay down as he wrenched the young man's hands around his back. "Derek Matthews, you're under arrest for evading a police officer and fleeing the scene of a crime."

"What crime?" Derek asked loudly in protest. "I didn't do nuthin'."

"Then why did you take off when you saw me?" Quinn demanded, patting the suspect's pockets. "Hmm, what do we have here? Is that marijuana and a pipe?"

"It's not mine," Derek claimed. "I borrowed these jeans from a friend."

"Yeah, right. Tell it to the judge," Quinn advised. If he had a nickel for every time he'd heard that excuse, he'd be a rich man. "Now you're under arrest for possession. And that's a parole violation."

Derek let out a stream of curses that Quinn ignored. Thank goodness he had his badge, cuffs and gun handy, or this could have ended very differently. After making sure Derek was securely contained, he flipped open his phone to call for back up.

Before he could dial, though, the wail of sirens filled the air and a campus police car squealed around the corner, lights flashing. Shanna must have called them when he'd taken off after Derek.

Then he frowned and glanced behind him. Sure enough, Shanna was standing about twenty yards behind him, her phone in her hand. He wanted to yell at her for leaving the safety of the car, but the arrival of two fellow police officers distracted him.

"I'm pretty sure there was a drug deal going down outside the commons," Quinn told Craig and Skip, the two guys who'd responded to Shanna's call. "This guy took off from the scene. I found drugs in his pocket, and his fingerprints have been discovered at the scene of Brady's murder. Not to mention he has a felony record for drug dealing in Wisconsin."

"Well, well, well," Craig drawled. "Looks like you've earned yourself a trip down to the cop shop."

"I didn't do nuthin'," Derek mumbled weakly, as if he sensed returning to jail might be imminent. "I wanna lawyer."

"Can you afford one? Or should we put a call in to the Public Defender's office?" Quinn asked.

The pained expression on Derek's face made it clear how he felt about the Public Defender's office, but he gave a resigned sigh. "I can't afford one."

"Then we'll call someone for you." Quinn didn't like how lawyers managed to get reduced or eliminated charges for criminals, releasing them back onto the streets, but in his heart he believed in the justice system. So Matthews would get his public defender.

"Murphy, you'll need to come downtown with us," Skip pointed out as he hauled Derek Matthews to his feet. "We'll need a formal statement regarding exactly what you saw."

Quinn glanced over to where Shanna still stood on the fringes of the group and gestured for her to come over. "That's fine, but Ms. Dawson is coming with me."

"Did you see anything?" Craig asked Shanna.

"Just how the group of kids scattered when they realized Quinn was about to bust them."

"We'll take your statement, too, just in case," Craig decided.

Quinn stepped back, giving room to Skip and Craig to take their suspect to the caged police cruiser. He took Shanna's hand in his as they walked back to his SUV. "I wish you would have stayed inside with the doors locked," he said.

"I know, Quinn. But when you took off after Derek, I saw Tanya Jacobs run straight for me, so I took a picture with my cell phone. I thought it might help if we could prove that both of them were there together."

"Good thinking," he praised her. "And I'm glad you didn't try to follow her."

"I was going to," Shanna admitted. "But then I decided I should back you up instead."

Back him up? There she went with that partner mentality again. Except she was a crime-scene investigator, which meant she was far removed from the type of action he faced every day. And his gut twisted at the thought of Shanna being anywhere near the danger he was accustomed to.

"Shanna, why is it that you keep forgetting there's some crazy stalker following you?" he asked, trying not to let his frustration show. "I can't help feeling that guy is going to strike out at you when we least expect it."

"I couldn't leave you to face Derek alone," she stubbornly repeated. "What if he'd had a gun?"

He stared at her, not sure what to say. He'd never met a woman like Shanna. One who was strong, stubborn, determined, yet didn't carry the hard edge that he'd noticed in many female cops.

The ride to the campus police headquarters didn't take long. They'd process Derek Matthews's paperwork there first, before sending him downtown.

Inside the station, there was the usual amount of chaos. He noticed Shanna looked around with keen curiosity. Before he could take her someplace to sit and wait, Hank Nelson strolled over.

"Holding out on me, Murphy?" he asked, a glint of anger in his eyes.

"No, sir. At least, that wasn't my intent. I'd like to fill you in on everything we've discovered so far. But first I need to give my statement regarding the drug bust."

Detective Nelson scowled and crossed his arms over his chest. "I'll wait."

He glanced over to find Craig, but he was still busy with their suspect. Skip was already taking Shanna's statement so he crossed over to his desk and booted up his computer to write down his version of the events.

Officer Craig arrived about ten minutes later, just as Quinn was finishing. He printed the document, then quickly went through everything verbally.

"What made you recognize the suspect?" Craig asked, when Quinn finished.

"His prints, along with Tanya Jacobs's prints, were found at Brady's crime scene," he admitted. Shanna had finished with Skip and came over to stand beside him.

"That's interesting," Craig murmured. "Okay, thanks. If we have more questions we'll let you know."

"Sounds good." He stood and looked at Shanna. "Detective Nelson wants to talk to us."

She grimaced a bit and nodded. "Yeah, he told me. We're supposed to meet him in the interview room, wherever that is."

"This way," he said, taking her arm. Hank stood there, still scowling, when they both took seats on the same side of the table.

So this is what it felt like to be interviewed like a suspect, he thought wryly, when Hank closed the door and dropped into a chair across from them.

He glanced at Shanna, whose expression radiated guilt, and took the lead. "Maybe we need to start at the beginning."

"Yeah. Why don't you?" Hank asked snidely.

So Quinn went through everything—Shanna's stalker, Brady's notes regarding the New Beginnings Adoption Agency, how Dennis Green was adopted through that agency, discovering Derek's and Tanya's fingerprints at the crime scene, looking for Skylar and the mysterious Phoebe, the two attacks on Shanna by her stalker and finishing with their theory that Dennis Green and Kenny Larson were the same person.

Shanna pulled out the computer image they'd printed at the university and slid it across the table toward Hank. "We thought at first that Brady's death was related to some sort of love triangle between Anna, Phoebe and Brady, but now we're thinking the New Beginnings Adoption Agency could be the common factor. They handled Dennis Green's adoption, placing a kidnapped child with a new family. Who knows how many other kidnappings could be related? My sister, Skylar, was kidnapped nine months after Kenny Larson. Can it be just one big coincidence that her fingerprints have shown up at the scene of Brady's crime, when Brady's roommate was kidnapped and adopted, too?"

Hank hadn't spoken more than a couple of terse

sentences during their long explanation of what they'd discovered. Quinn sensed the detective was still angry, but after Shanna's passionate question, he sighed heavily.

"I'm still mad at both of you, but you're right. This isn't a coincidence. If we're dealing with kidnappings that happened fourteen and fifteen years ago, then I need to get the FBI involved."

"I promise, we really were planning to come to you with this information," Quinn said. "The drug deal going down at the corner of the commons distracted me."

Hank tossed them both a look full of skepticism.

"Honestly, we were," Shanna spoke up earnestly. "I know we need the FBI to help find Skylar, and you must realize how badly I want to find my sister."

"Okay, okay," Hank said, throwing his hands up in the air. "Quit groveling already. I'll make the call to the feds, but you both have to promise me to stay out of this from now on. We can't work this case in a vacuum."

"But—" Shanna started, and he grabbed her hand under the table and squeezed it as a warning to keep quiet.

There was a sharp knock at the door and Hank turned around. "Yeah?" he called.

The door opened and Craig poked his head in. "Murphy, you're not going to believe this. We matched Matthews's fingerprints to one of your open cases."

One of his open cases? "Which one?"

Craig pushed the door open and tossed some papers onto the table in front of Quinn. "Remember that robbery at the Corner Café a few months ago?"

"Yeah. I remember." The night was etched in his mind as one of the few times in his job as a campus cop that he'd been forced to fire his gun. "The suspect got away, and we found his escape vehicle, which happened to be stolen, a few miles from the café."

"Yeah, and when we recovered the gun and the car, we found a partial print on the steering wheel. The print matches your drug-dealing suspect, Derek Matthews."

Quinn frowned. "Matthews has a record. We didn't match him earlier?"

"We did, but we'd canvassed the area without anyone claiming to recognize him," Craig explained. "Now that he's been brought in for possession, we can hold him on the armed-robbery charge, too."

Quinn was glad of that, since the young girl behind the counter at the café, who'd looked tough with her purple-streaked hair and her eyebrow piercing, had been badly shaken after the robbery. He remembered far too clearly how she'd broken down and sobbed on his shoulder.

"He's going back to prison for sure this time," Craig said with satisfaction.

"That's good," Quinn murmured. Glancing down at the police report, a familiar name jumped out at him, and he stared down in amazement. The name of the victim, the girl with the purple-streaked hair who'd been robbed at gunpoint by Derek Matthews, had the same first name as their mystery girl.

Phoebe Fontaine.

TWELVE

Quinn dragged his gaze from Phoebe's name on the police report to look at Shanna. He wanted to let her know he might have found their mystery girl, but truthfully he wasn't even sure Phoebe was still working at the Corner Café. Although with a last name, they should be able to find a last known address.

He didn't say anything out loud, though, because while he understood Hank's desire to take the lead in the investigation, he wanted to follow up on this lead himself. They'd already given Hank everything they had, including Kyle's claim that Anna was jealous of how Brady was supposedly "flirting" with a girl named Phoebe.

Hank was going to get the feds involved, which was good because the FBI had a better chance of following up on all adoptions handled through the New Beginnings Adoption Agency. And with Dennis Green matching the photo of missing four-year-old Kenny Larson, there was a good chance his brother's murder was linked to his proposed newspaper article.

For some reason, he wanted to give Shanna a chance to see Phoebe first, meet with her, talk to her. They'd already decided that it was hardly likely that Phoebe was really Skylar, but he wanted to make sure before he turned the information over to Hank and the feds.

"Quinn? Anything else you want to add?" Hank asked.

He dragged his attention back to the current discussion. "I'm sorry, what was the question?"

Hank gave an exasperated sigh. "We're going to start following up on the Dennis Green/Kenny Larson angle, and call the feds to see where they want to go from here. Do you agree with the plan?"

His approval wasn't necessary; Hank could really do whatever he wanted, but Quinn appreciated being allowed to participate. "I think it's a good plan," he said, glancing at Shanna. "We desperately want to find Shanna's missing sister, Skylar."

"And we want to know who killed Brady," Shanna added.

"Don't worry, the more pieces to the puzzle we

uncover, the more likely we'll find the missing links," Hank assured her.

"If you don't need anything more from us, we'd like to get going," Quinn said, rising to his feet. "We've missed lunch, and I don't know about Shanna, but I can't think clearly on an empty stomach."

Hank's gaze narrowed suspiciously, but then he slowly nodded. "We're finished here, but if anything else happens I want you to call me ASAP."

"We will," Shanna assured him.

Quinn took her hand as they strolled outside, crossing the street to the parking lot where he'd left his car. After they were both seated inside, he started the car and looked at Shanna. "I think I found Phoebe."

Her blue eyes widened in shock. "What? When? How?"

"She works at the Corner Café, or at least she did at the time of the robbery." He backed out of the parking space and then took a right-hand turn, heading toward the café. "Phoebe Fontaine was the girl working behind the counter the night Derek Matthews tried to rob her."

"Thank You, God," Shanna whispered reverently. "I've been praying we'd find her."

"Shanna, don't get your hopes up too high," he cautioned as he took a left at the next stoplight.

"We don't know that Phoebe is adopted, and we certainly don't know that she's Skylar."

Shanna nodded quickly, but he could still see the frank hope reflected in her eyes. "I know, Quinn. Trust me—I do realize that this is a total stretch. But what if she is Skylar? What if today is the day I'm going to find my missing sister?"

Luckily, he managed to find a parking spot just a couple of blocks down from the Corner Café. He turned off the engine and twisted in the seat to face Shanna. "I'll be thrilled if you do find your missing sister. Before we go inside, though, you need to know how Phoebe looked the last time I saw her."

Shanna's smile evaporated and she clasped her hands together tightly in her lap. "What do you mean how she looked? Is she in trouble? On drugs? In an abusive relationship? What?"

"No, Shanna, she was physically fine, from what I could tell. Shaken after being held up at gunpoint, but fine."

She let out an audible sigh of relief. "Well, what are you talking about then?"

"Just that she doesn't have the sweet, girl-next-door look. Phoebe has dark hair heavily streaked with purple and an eyebrow piercing."

Shanna hiked her eyebrows upward. "So what? Do you think I care if she has purple hair or facial piercings? If she's my sister, I'll accept her no matter how she looks."

He grinned with relief. "Okay, then. Let's go."

Shanna was so excited, she wanted to sprint at full speed rather than walk calmly beside Quinn as they followed the sidewalk to the Corner Café.

She took several deep breaths, reminding herself that it was far more likely that Phoebe wasn't Skylar. But even a one percent chance was better than nothing.

They walked inside the café, which was surprisingly crowded. Going from the bright sunlight outside to the darker interior of the café momentarily blinded her. She stood for several seconds until her eyes adjusted to less light.

"Do you see her?" she asked in a low tone, searching for anyone with purple-streaked hair. Although for all they knew, Phoebe could have changed to blue or green streaks, or none at all. If she'd turned blonde, would Quinn still recognize her?

"Not yet, but let's find a seat first," Quinn answered, sweeping the area with his gaze.

Shanna noticed two girls rising to their feet from a small table near the back of the café. She darted around several students standing and talking to snatch the vacant table.

Quinn followed her but didn't sit down. "What would you like?" he asked. "Are you hungry? They have some muffins and other baked goods for sale, too."

"Coffee and a muffin would be great."

Quinn stood in line, and she watched the two girls behind the counter closely, searching for any possible similarities to Skylar.

It wasn't easy to get a good look though, since there were so many people milling about the café, and the two counter attendants kept turning their backs to fill orders. She should have offered to go up for the coffee and muffins.

Quinn returned five minutes later with their order. Before she could open her mouth to ask, he shook his head. "No, Phoebe isn't working right now. She's due to come in at four o'clock."

"Four o'clock?" she echoed with a stab of disappointment. "That's over an hour from now."

"I know," Quinn said as he sat down in the chair across from hers. "But we're probably better off waiting here. Unless you have a better idea?"

"No, I don't have a better idea," she admitted.

Quinn quickly unwrapped his muffin and then hesitated, glancing up at her. "We should pray first, right?"

She laughed, the tension easing out of her chest. She should know better than to try and rush God's plan. She'd find Skylar when God intended, and not before. "Yes, we should."

He reached over to take her hand and then bowed his head. She held his hand and closed her eyes, praying in a low voice just loud enough for Quinn to hear. "Dear Lord, thank You for providing us food to eat, and please keep us safe and show us the path You want us to take. We also ask that You continue to keep Skylar safe in Your care. Amen."

"Amen," Quinn echoed.

"Next time, it's your turn to provide the prayer," she teased as she removed the cellophane from her muffin. They weren't freshly baked, but she was so hungry she didn't care. And the muffins were surprisingly good.

"I'll try," he said hesitantly. "But I still have a lot to learn."

"You'll be fine." She paused, glancing around the café. "We probably should have told Hank we were coming here," she murmured before taking a sip of her coffee. "I don't think he's very happy with us."

Quinn shrugged. "Look, Shanna, we don't know that Phoebe has anything to do with Brady's murder or the mystery surrounding your sister's disappearance. As soon as we know something, I promise to call Hank. Besides, we did tell him about Kyle Ryker's accusations regarding Anna being upset with Brady for flirting with Phoebe, remember?"

"Yes, but we didn't tell him Phoebe works here at the Corner Café."

"We didn't know that for sure until we came and asked for her," Quinn pointed out. "She could have easily quit her job here after being held up at gunpoint."

"True," she admitted with a frown. "I wonder why she stayed? This can't be the only job around. And since she's not enrolled in any classes, she wouldn't be limited to something on campus. And surely her parents would have encouraged her to find something different, don't you think?"

"Yes, assuming her parents knew about the incident."

"I suppose you're right." She didn't want to think about Phoebe being estranged from her parents. Guiltily, she realized that the main reason she didn't want to believe Phoebe was estranged from her parents was because she believed Phoebe could be Skylar.

"Don't look now, but Anna and Maggie just walked in," Quinn said in a low, urgent tone.

She almost turned to look, despite his warning not to. Keeping her gaze on his, she leaned toward him. "Should we go over to talk to them?" she asked.

"I don't want to scare Anna off again, but I would like to talk to her," Quinn admitted.

From the corner of her eye, she could see both girls, Maggie and a brunette who she assumed was Anna, standing in line at the counter. "If we're going to talk to them, we should head over by the door so Anna can't take off running again."

"Exactly what I was thinking," he admitted. "Let's wait until they've placed their order."

The next three minutes passed with excruciating slowness. It was hard not to stare at Maggie and Anna, so she kept her eyes locked on Quinn's.

Finally he rose smoothly to his feet, and she quickly followed him as he made his way through the cramped maze of tables to the front door.

Once Maggie and Anna had their respective coffees, they turned to walk toward the door. The shocked expression on Maggie's and Anna's faces and the way they stopped abruptly was almost comical.

Maggie was the first to recover, but the terrified expression on Anna's face tugged at her heart. What on earth caused the girl to be so afraid? Instinctively, Shanna stepped forward in an attempt to reassure her. "Please don't panic, Anna. We just want to talk to you. I promise you're not in trouble or anything. We just have a few questions."

"Just talk to them, Anna," Maggie urged with obvious exasperation. "They'll find you eventually anyway."

"I already gave my statement to the police. I don't have anything more to tell you," Anna argued with a dark scowl. "Why can't you just leave me alone?"

Something was off; the fear radiating from the girl was nearly palpable. "What's wrong, Anna? Is someone bothering you? What are you so afraid of?"

Anna didn't answer, but the slight flicker in her gaze gave her away.

"We shouldn't talk here," Quinn pointed out, as a few café patrons were beginning to watch them with interest. He stared at Anna. "We can do this the easy way or the hard way," he said conversationally. "We can go outside and talk in private, or I can arrest you now and we can talk down at the station. Your choice. And know this—if we go outside and you take off running, the latter option automatically takes precedence."

"Come on, Anna," Maggie urged. "Let's just get this over with, okay?"

"Fine." Anna angled her chin stubbornly and waited for Quinn to hold the door open before moving past them to go outside. For a moment, the girl's stubbornness reminded Shanna of how she was at that age.

Could Anna be Skylar? The hair color was right, as was the age. Her pulse kicked into high gear at the possibility.

But once they were outside, standing alongside the brick building of the café, she realized Anna's eyes were a greenish hazel, not brown. No colored contacts, either. Her heart sank like a rock.

"So what do you want to know?" Anna demanded. Her spunk in the face of her earlier fear was admirable.

"You come to this café often?" Quinn asked casually.

Anna shrugged. "Sometimes, why?"

"You must know Phoebe then, right?" Quinn asked again.

Anna's mouth thinned. "No, I don't know her. I heard she works here, but I could care less about that."

"Really? You didn't care that Brady spent so much time hanging out here?" Quinn pressed.

"Not really," Anna said, although the guarded expression in her eyes made Shanna think the girl did mind, very much. "I don't care what you've heard. I know Brady loved me."

Love? A pretty strong word for a twenty-year-old. "I'm sure he did care about you," Shanna said with a smile. "Which is why it makes perfect sense that you'd be upset to find out he was flirting with someone else."

Anna refused to acknowledge the obvious. "You can believe whatever you want. I don't care."

"So what happened last night?" Quinn asked, changing the subject. "Why did you take off running when you saw us?"

"I wasn't in the mood to be interrogated," Anna shot back. "Why is it so hard for you to understand I just want to be left alone?"

"Anna, why don't you tell them?" Maggie asked in a low tone. "He's a cop. Maybe he can help."

Shanna glanced at Quinn, who looked as puzzled as she felt. "Anna, what's wrong? What's going on?"

"Nothing," Anna said, shrugging off Maggie's hand.

"Some old guy was bothering her," Maggie announced. "That's why she's been trying to stay low-key."

A chill snaked down Shanna's back. Could the old guy bothering Anna be the same guy who'd been stalking her? And if so, why?

"It's nothing," Anna insisted. "I haven't seen him in a week. It was probably just my imagination anyway."

"Can you give me a description?" Quinn asked, a frown furrowing his brow.

Anna shrugged. "Not very tall, about five feet ten inches with gray hair."

"Could you work with a sketch artist, maybe?" Shanna suggested.

"No, I didn't really get a good look at him. Besides, I told you, I haven't seen him in a while."

"Where do you work?" Shanna persisted.

"At the Olive Grove restaurant," Maggie supplied on her friend's behalf. "She's a hostess there during the week."

"Lately, I've only been working a couple of shifts each week," Anna admitted. "Because of the rehearsals and the play."

"You're sure you can't give us any more description of the guy following you?" Quinn asked.

"I'm sure."

Shanna caught Quinn's gaze and shrugged. She didn't know what else to do to encourage the young woman to open up.

"Can I go now?" Anna asked. "My coffee's getting cold."

"Yes. But Anna, if you see that old guy following you again, will you please call me?" Quinn took out his wallet, extracted a business card and handed one to Anna. "Please? I don't want you to get hurt."

Anna took Quinn's card with obvious reluctance. "All right," she agreed slowly. "If I see Creepy Guy again, I'll call you."

"Thanks," Quinn murmured.

Shanna watched thoughtfully as Maggie and Anna hurried away. "Do you think it's possible we have the same stalker?"

"Anything is possible," Quinn responded grimly. "But it's weird that he'd leave you notes and break into your home to attack you while doing nothing more than following Anna around."

"She has hazel eyes," she said, a hint of sadness in her tone. "So she can't be Skylar."

"I know." Quinn put his arm around her shoulders, surprising her with a quick embrace. "Don't worry, I just know we're going to find Skylar."

She raised her gaze to his. "I hope so," she whispered.

For a long moment he gazed down at her, and she sensed he wanted to kiss her. She held her breath, surprised by how much she wanted it, too, but then the moment was gone.

"It's past four," Quinn said, dropping his arm and stepping away. "Let's go meet Phoebe."

She nodded, trying to hide her disappointment. Surely meeting Phoebe, seeing if she was actually Skylar, was more important than Quinn's kiss?

Of course it was.

Back inside the café, they walked up to the counter. The place had emptied out; there was no line. "Could we please speak to Phoebe Fontaine?" Quinn asked.

"Sorry, but Phoebe called in sick," the young girl behind the counter said. "She sounded terrible."

Sick? Shanna frowned and glanced doubtfully at Quinn.

"Okay, thanks for letting us know," he said pleasantly. He turned and headed for the door, and she quickly followed, swallowing the hard lump of disappointment.

"I'm so upset," she said as they walked back toward Quinn's SUV. "I really wanted to talk to her."

Quinn flipped open his cell phone and punched in a number. "Hi, Skip. Do me a favor and pull up Phoebe Fontaine's address for me."

By the time they reached the car, Quinn had Phoebe's address. As much as she felt bad bothering the poor girl when she was sick, Shanna didn't protest when he drove the few blocks to a rather run-down apartment building.

"Phoebe lives here?" she asked, trying to hide her dismay.

"Apartment 217," Quinn said, climbing out from behind the wheel.

They walked up to the main door, and Quinn frowned when he tugged on it. "I can't believe it's not locked," he muttered.

There was a small foyer with mailboxes lining one wall. The door leading to the rest of the building was locked. He pushed the intercom button above number 217 and waited.

No answer. Shanna stepped up and pushed the buzzer a second time, holding the button in longer. But still there was no answer.

"I can't believe it," Shanna murmured.

Quinn rubbed a hand over his chin. "I guess we'll have to come back tomorrow."

She stared at the silver mailbox with the name Fontaine printed neatly above it. "Maybe not," she said, as an idea formed. "What if I dusted her mailbox for fingerprints? If we're able to match Phoebe's prints to the ones we have on file for Skylar, we'd know for sure that they're the same person." Shanna gazed at Quinn, barely able to contain her excitement. She was so close to proving Phoebe was really Skylar, and she didn't want to wait one minute longer than she had to in order to prove it.

THIRTEEN

"I doubt you'll get anything useful," Quinn protested.

She lightly grasped his arm. "Please, Quinn? What can it hurt to *try?* I can't bear not knowing for sure."

He glanced down at her and then smiled slowly. "All right, Shanna," he agreed. "Why not?"

"Great." She was overwhelmed with relief. "Take me back to my place—I have everything I need at home."

Quinn nodded, and they left the apartment building where Phoebe lived to walk back to his SUV.

"Don't get your hopes up too high," he cautioned as he drove toward her house. "We have no proof whatsoever that Phoebe is Skylar."

"I know," Shanna murmured. And she did know the odds were against them. At the same time, she couldn't completely quell her excitement. She knew God was helping her, showing her the way. And if the fingerprints weren't a match, then she'd know to keep moving forward.

When Quinn pulled into her driveway, she gripped the door handle, ready to bolt into the house.

"Hold it," Quinn commanded, hitting the locks so she couldn't jump out of the car. "You're not going inside until I make sure it's safe."

"All right," she said, handing over her keys. "But please hurry." Holding back wasn't easy, but there wasn't any point in arguing. The faster Quinn determined no one was hiding inside, the quicker she'd get her supplies and head back to Phoebe's apartment.

"Stay inside the car with the doors locked," Quinn instructed. She waited until he'd climbed out from behind the wheel before hitting the door locks.

Quinn went inside and she held her breath, fidgeting impatiently in her seat as she waited for him to return. After a long, agonizing ten minutes, he finally opened the door and gestured for her to come inside.

"Doesn't seem like anyone's been in since you were here last," Quinn admitted as he held the door open for her. "The air is a bit stale."

She wrinkled her nose, agreeing with his

assessment. Surely by now, the stalker had given up watching her house, especially given that she hadn't been back to stay since the night of the attack.

In her closet, she found her fingerprint kit right where she'd left it, tucked in a corner in the back. She brought it out and walked back to the kitchen. "Quinn, I really need to take my car back to the university campus. This investigation is heating up, and I don't want to be without my own vehicle."

"No, absolutely not." The stubborn expression on Quinn's face made her want to sigh.

"Quinn, we can cover more ground on this investigation if we each have our own cars." She knew she was fighting an uphill battle, but she had to try. "Besides, I'm sure the stalker has given up watching my house and my car, since we purposefully haven't used them in the past few days."

"What about the attempted hit-and-run?" Quinn asked skeptically.

"We don't even know that I was the target," she pointed out. "And he probably got lucky catching sight of me walking along the street. I'll be safer in a vehicle."

Quinn stared at her for a long moment. "I'll only agree on one condition."

"What's that?"

"We switch vehicles for now. I'll drive your car and you can drive mine."

At least he'd attempted to compromise, meeting her halfway. "Agreed. Thanks, Quinn."

"You're welcome," he responded grudgingly.

They swapped car keys, and Shanna waited on the street in Quinn's car until he'd pulled her car out of the driveway and closed the garage door behind him.

He went ahead, and she followed behind as they drove back to Carlyle University. Finding two parking spaces next to Phoebe's apartment wasn't easy, but Quinn didn't say anything about it as they walked up to the apartment building.

Shanna eagerly began to unpack her supplies, but Quinn once again pushed the buzzer for Phoebe's apartment. She froze, holding her breath, but just as earlier, there was no answer.

"If she's sick, why isn't she here to answer the door?" he muttered under his breath.

"Maybe she went home to visit her parents," she mused, brushing the silver metal door with fingerprint powder. "She's still young—maybe she's looking for some TLC from her mother while she's not feeling good."

"Maybe," Quinn responded, although he didn't look convinced.

She worked on the mailbox door, but after a

good ten minutes, she tossed the brush down in disgust. "You were right, Quinn. There are way too many prints on this door to find anything useful."

"It was worth a try," he said consolingly.

She didn't want to admit defeat. Taking a soft cloth from her kit, she wiped down the door, using force to make sure that all the current smudges were eliminated. "Maybe when she returns home, she'll check her mail and I'll be able to find an isolated print." Tonight. She'd come back later tonight.

Quinn's cell phone rang before he could respond. "Hi, Hank," he answered. "What's up?" There was a long pause, and then he met her gaze. "Yeah, she's here with me. I'll let her know, thanks."

She lifted a brow. "Let me know what?"

"That Special Agent Marc Tanner from the FBI wants to talk to you. Actually, to both of us."

She shouldn't have been surprised. Hadn't Hank told them he was getting the feds involved? "That was fast," she murmured.

"Yeah and they're waiting down at the police station, anxious for us to tell them everything we know," Quinn said.

She glanced regretfully at the shiny silver mailbox and then forced herself to turn away. She would come back after their meeting with the feds. "Well then, I guess we shouldn't keep them waiting any longer."

Quinn pulled up into the police station general parking lot and waited for Shanna to park his SUV in the empty spot next to him. He tried to tell himself that Shanna was perfectly safe in his vehicle, rather than driving around in her own, but knowing that logically didn't prevent him from offering a quick, silent prayer.

Dear God, please keep Shanna safe in Your care.

He found the prayer comforting, and knew that Shanna deserved the credit for his newfound faith. The way her blue eyes sparkled bright with excitement made her look more beautiful than ever.

Once again, he wondered what would happen between the two of them once they'd found Shanna's sister and Brady's killer. The case had brought them together, but once it was solved, would they each go their separate ways?

He knew that being a cop made having a relationship nearly impossible, but now that he'd met Shanna, he didn't want to lose her.

She's not yours to lose, he reminded himself sternly. But he still took her elbow as they walked up the stairs and into the station.

Hank stood beside a tall, young man with chocolate-brown hair and clean-cut features. For a moment, he glanced down at Shanna, hoping she didn't find the guy attractive. She must have sensed his gaze because she glanced up at him and smiled nervously.

"Thanks for coming in so quickly," Hank said by way of greeting. "Special Agent Marc Tanner, this is Officer Quinn Murphy and crime-scene investigator Shanna Dawson."

"Nice to meet you," Shanna said, stepping forward to take Agent Tanner's outstretched hand. "Skylar Dawson is my younger sister."

"Ms. Dawson. Officer Murphy." Agent Marc Tanner shook hands with both of them briefly and didn't waste any time on small talk. "If you'll come this way?" He indicated the room they'd occupied just a few hours earlier.

The way Shanna clasped her hands tightly in her lap betrayed her nervousness. He put a hand on her back, trying to reassure her. They took two seats across the table from Agent Tanner.

"Officer Murphy, I understand you have some information regarding the New Beginnings Adoption Agency?" Agent Tanner asked.

"Yes. My brother, Brady Wallace, was doing a story on adoption for the university online newspaper. According to his notes, his roommate,

Dennis Green, had asked my brother to assist in finding his birth mother."

"Brady Wallace is your half brother, correct?" Agent Tanner asked.

Quinn tried not to let his annoyance show. "Technically, yes, we have different fathers. But Brady was my brother in every way that counts."

Agent Tanner looked surprised by his curt reaction. "I wasn't implying otherwise, Officer Murphy, just making sure I understood the difference in your last names."

He forced himself to relax. "Brady was looking for the New Beginnings Adoption Agency because that's the paperwork Dennis Green apparently had regarding his adoption. But the agency was only in business for five years. According to Brady's records, the agency shut its doors fourteen years ago."

"Interesting timing, wouldn't you agree?" Tanner asked. When Quinn nodded, the FBI agent continued, "Do you mind sharing all the information your brother uncovered for his article? He could have some information there that might seem innocuous but could in reality be a great lead."

"I don't mind at all, but honestly there isn't a lot of concrete information in his notes." Privately, Quinn had thought his brother hadn't exactly used the unbiased eye of a journalist on the subject. But Brady was only a journalism major, not a full-fledged investigative reporter. "Most of the stuff he wrote down was nothing more than theory and speculation. Although he was trying to find other private-adoption agencies that were in the area, too."

This caused Agent Tanner to lean forward eagerly. "Do you have names of any other adoption agencies?"

He shook his head. "Sorry, but no, my brother didn't list any by name."

"I see." Disappointment flared in Tanner's eyes. "Well even so, I'd appreciate access to everything your brother has."

"I'll make sure you get a copy of this," he said, pulling out the jump drive.

Shanna had been quiet up until now. "Agent Tanner, do you have any leads on Skylar's disappearance? Is it possible she was also adopted out through the New Beginnings Adoption Agency?"

The FBI agent's gaze softened a bit. "Not yet, but you need to know, finding your sister's fingerprints at the crime scene injected life into a very cold case, Ms. Dawson. To be honest, we assumed your sister was dead."

Shanna blanched but nodded her understanding.

Quinn leaned forward, placing a reassuring arm around her shoulders. "We'll find her, Shanna," he murmured. "Knowing your sister is alive, is all that matters right now."

She nodded, but leaned against him anyway, as if needing some of his strength. He found he enjoyed being there for Shanna.

And maybe, just maybe, once they solved this case, she'd let him stay a part of her life.

The thought was a little scary, considering he'd given up any hope of ever having a relationship. But the alternative, life without Shanna, was even worse, so he squelched the niggle of fear.

"Obviously, we were hoping you had a few leads related to Skylar's kidnapping," Quinn said.

Agent Tanner was silent for a moment. "We do have an adoption agency that we're looking into right now that's located in Atlanta, Georgia. In fact, that's where I was when we got the call from your Detective Nelson. The name of the agency in Georgia is Sunrise Adoption Agency."

Shanna glanced up at Quinn hopefully, but he only shook his head. "Never heard of it, I'm afraid."

"Me, neither," Shanna said sadly.

"The founder of the agency is a guy named Geoff Wellington," Tanner continued. "And interestingly enough, the owner of the New Beginnings Agency was a man by the name of George Worth."

"The same initials, huh?" Quinn glanced at Shanna, who wore a hopeful expression. "Do you think these two could be the same guy?"

"We have photos of each man, and they don't look as if they're the same guy. But that doesn't mean that a ring of thieves hasn't figured out how to use fake names and identities, switching off as agency founders so no one links them together."

Quinn had to admit the theory made some sense. Criminals spent almost as much time covering their tracks as they did perpetuating actual crimes.

"So they really could be the same agency?" Shanna asked.

"This new agency has only been in business for eighteen months, so it's entirely possible that they keep reinventing themselves every few years," Tanner explained. "We've had our eye on them because within the past six months, two children within a fifty-mile radius of Atlanta have gone missing. And there were also two others, one from North Carolina and one from Alabama, who went missing. We suspect they're trying to widen the range of abductions to remove any potential links between the kidnappings."

Shanna reached over to grasp Quinn's hand tightly. "Four more? You have to stop them, Agent Tanner. Before any more children go missing."

"That's the plan, Ms. Dawson," he said with a hint of dryness in his tone. "But we're also trying to link this founder to the other agencies that are no longer in business. We're pretty sure that Geoff Wellington is an alias. He didn't exist, from what we can tell, until three years ago. And interestingly enough, George Worth disappeared right after New Beginnings closed down."

Quinn had to believe the feds were on the right track. "More evidence, although circumstantial, that they might be one and the same man."

"That's my thought," Tanner agreed.

"Is there anything we can do to help?" Quinn asked. He didn't want to be left out of the investigation, and he especially didn't want Shanna left out. She had more to lose. He wanted to bring justice to Brady's murderer, but she wanted to find her sister. Live siblings took priority over deceased ones.

"Not at this time. Trust me when I tell you we're following up on all leads," Tanner said kindly. "In fact, I'm going to interview Dennis Green next."

"I'm sure Hank told you we believe Dennis Green is really Kenny Larson, the child who disappeared from the shopping mall fifteen years ago," Shanna interjected. "I have the age-progression photo next to Dennis Green's university ID photo to prove it."

Agent Tanner's face darkened, as if he was embarrassed. "Yes, Detective Nelson did give us your photos. Nice piece of detective work, Ms. Dawson. Between finding your sister's fingerprints at Officer Murphy's brother's crime scene and discovering the link between Dennis Green and Kenny Larson, you've really helped us rejuvenate this cold case."

Quinn beamed with pride. Because he, too, thought Shanna had made remarkable strides in a case that was fourteen years old. "Maybe you should offer her a job," he joked.

Tanner didn't laugh or even crack a smile. "Maybe we should," he admitted grimly. "The agent in charge of this case retired a few years ago, and I can't say I'm overly impressed with his efforts."

"Interesting," Quinn murmured. He bet there was plenty of finger-pointing going around at the FBI headquarters now that a lowly college journalism student and a crime-scene investigator had broken their case wide open.

"I'd ask you to both stay in touch with me, especially if you find out anything further," Tanner continued, sliding two business cards across the table.

"Of course," Shanna murmured.

He pocketed Tanner's card and then removed his arm from Shanna's shoulder, immediately missing the warmth of her skin and the vanilla scent she wore. "We'd appreciate you keeping us in the loop, too, especially if you find out anything about Shanna's sister."

Tanner's smile resembled a pained grimace. "Guess that's the least I can do after the way you've helped us out."

He and Shanna shook the agent's hand again before leaving. Outside, he noticed a young man with a sullen expression on his face sitting beside Hank Nelson.

Recognizing Dennis Green from his photo, he gave his brother's roommate a brief nod before making his way to the door. Shanna followed much more slowly, hardly able to tear her gaze away from the boy she believed to be Kenny Larson.

"Are you okay?" he asked in a low voice as they walked out to their respective vehicles.

"I just can't help thinking how happy his family will be to see him," she admitted slowly. "But he already has a life, and adopted parents who love him. He wanted to find his birth mother, but discovering he was really kidnapped must be a shock. I'm just realizing how difficult it will be for him to reconcile his two identities."

He knew she was talking about Skylar more so than Dennis Green. "Shanna, don't think the worst. Not yet. Skylar is alive, which is more than you've hoped for over the years, isn't it?"

"Yes, it is." She stopped beside his SUV, glancing up at him. "I'm sorry, Quinn. I don't know what's wrong with me. I should be happy that Skylar is alive and well. If she doesn't want me in her life, then I'll learn to live with that."

Would she really? He wasn't at all convinced. "I'm sure that in time, Dennis Green and Skylar will come around."

"I know," she said quickly. But there was a faint glitter of tears in her eyes.

"Shanna," he murmured, hating to see her upset. "Don't cry. Please don't cry."

"I'm not," she protested, even as she sniffled.

Unable to stand her suffering for another second, he drew her into his arms and lowered his head to capture her mouth in a gentle kiss.

FOURTEEN

Momentarily surprised by Quinn's kiss, it took a second for her to respond. This kiss was different, more deliberate than the first one. When she felt him begin to pull away, she quickly wrapped her arms around his neck to stop him, holding him close and trying to tell him, without words, to stay.

He obliged her by kissing her again, and her brief sadness over Skylar was quickly replaced by overwhelming feelings for Quinn. He tasted wonderful, and she'd been dreaming about this moment since the first time he'd kissed her.

All too soon, the lingering kiss was over and she clung to his shoulders, worried her boneless legs wouldn't hold her weight.

"Shanna," he murmured again, his face buried in her hair and his arms wrapped tightly around her waist. She loved the way he said her name. The way his heart pounded in his chest beneath her ear made her feel good to know he was as affected by that kiss as she was. "I hope you're not looking for an apology."

She laughed weakly and shook her head, wishing they could stay like this forever. "No, Quinn. I'm not looking for an apology." In fact, she wondered what he'd think if she asked him to kiss her again.

"We'd better get going," he said with true regret, but he didn't move. Clearly he was waiting for her to decide where to go from here.

She didn't want their embrace to end, but they were standing in the middle of the parking lot, and besides, she really did want to go back to Phoebe's apartment building to see if there were any fingerprints on the surface of the mailbox. Prints that didn't belong to the postman, that is.

"I guess we'd better," she agreed, loosening her grip. Strength returned to her limbs as her heart rate slowed to normal. The moment she pulled away, he released her.

His gaze searched hers and she smiled, feeling her cheeks turn warm. Her fair skin made it difficult to hide her feelings.

"You're so beautiful, Shanna," Quinn said in a low, rough tone. "I don't deserve someone as good and kindhearted as you."

She thought that was an odd choice of words.

"That's funny, because I was just thinking we deserved each other."

A shadow darkened his green eyes, and he turned to open the driver's side door of his SUV. "Where are you heading off to?" he asked, completely changing the subject. "I have to make a copy of Brady's notes for Agent Tanner, but then I can meet you back at the coffee shop, or Karly's Kitchen if you want to grab something to eat."

She wanted to ask why he didn't think he deserved happiness, but sensed he wasn't going to open up about the topic here and now. Maybe later they could eat dinner and talk. "Karly's Kitchen is probably a good idea. We already know Phoebe isn't returning to the Corner Café tonight. How about we meet in an hour? I'm going to check Phoebe's mailbox for fingerprints first."

"Shanna." The exasperation in his tone was clear. "Don't set yourself up to be disappointed."

She knew he was only trying to help, but she didn't appreciate the way he kept bursting her bubble. "If that happens, it's my problem, isn't it?" she said curtly as she slid behind the wheel. She reached over to close the door, but he hung on to it.

"I'm sorry," he said with a sigh, sensing her annoyance. "I really do hope you're right and that you find something significant."

She couldn't help thinking Quinn was the type of man who hedged his bets. The type who didn't get his hopes up so he wouldn't be disappointed. Maybe because he'd been hurt in the past? "I'll see you in an hour, okay?" she said, forcing a smile.

He hesitated, and then stepped back and released the door. Quinn stood watching her as she started the car and then backed out of the parking spot.

Leaving him standing there felt strange. She hadn't been left alone much the past few days. With Quinn driving her around and helping her, she'd gotten used to his presence.

About time she stood on her own two feet. Quinn wasn't going to be with her forever. Once they'd found Skylar and the person who'd killed his brother, they'd likely go their separate ways.

She lightly touched her lips, still tingling from Quinn's kiss. Maybe they wouldn't go their separate ways. Maybe this time, he'd kissed her as a way to tell her he wanted to keep seeing her even once this investigation was over.

The thought made her smile.

And even the sharp disappointment, fifteen minutes later, of not finding any fingerprints on Phoebe's mailbox didn't wipe the smile off her face.

* * *

Quinn couldn't get Shanna's voice out of his head as he used his computer at work to make a copy of Brady's notes for Agent Tanner.

That's funny, because I was thinking we deserved each other.

For a moment his heart had leaped with excitement, before it crashed to the pit of his stomach. That was easy for her to say, since Shanna didn't know everything about him. She didn't have a clue how close he was to making the same mistakes his father had made.

He dropped off the removable storage disk for Agent Tanner and then decided to go back to the coffee shop to chat with Brady's friends before heading over to meet Shanna.

There was no point wishing his life had been different. But he did wish that he could be the man Shanna thought he was.

Lost in thought as he walked up to the Corner Café, he almost missed the flash of purple hair. As soon as he realized the girl ahead of him might be Phoebe, he broke into a run.

Thankfully, she was just as oblivious because he caught up to her easily enough. "Phoebe?" he asked urgently.

She turned around in surprise, her gaze narrowing with suspicion when she saw him. "Leave me alone!" she cried.

"Wait! Please, don't run." Keeping one hand up where she could see it, he reached into his breast pocket to pull out his badge. "You're not in any trouble, I promise. I just want to ask a few questions, okay?"

She didn't run, but stood glaring at him. And then she sneezed twice in a row.

"Bless you," he said automatically.

"Thanks," she muttered, sniffling loudly and digging in her pocket for a tissue. "Better stay back—I'm full of germs."

"Is that why you called off your shift?" he asked, tempted to call Shanna but worried he might scare Phoebe away if he did.

"Yeah." She blew her nose loudly. With her puffy eyes, red nose and purple hair, it was hard for him to tell if Phoebe bore any resemblance to Shanna—if she could possibly by Skylar. "Have you ever tried serving customers when your nose is running like a faucet and you keep sneezing and coughing? Mega gross."

He chuckled, enjoying her self-deprecating sense of humor. "I completely understand. Look, I know you're not feeling well, but a friend of mine wants to meet you and ask you a couple of questions if you don't mind."

Her gaze turned wary. "Is this about Brady?"

"Yes." He kept his tone light, casual, so she wouldn't take off. "Did you know Brady Wallace?"

She nodded, her eyes filling with pain. "He came into the café all the time. We became close friends."

It was on the tip of his tongue to ask just how close they were, but he kept his questions non-threatening for now. "I'm sure his death must have been hard for you."

"Very," she said in a low whisper. "I cared about him a lot."

Her sorrow seemed genuine. "Did you attend his party that night?" he asked. His phone was in his pocket, and with a casual movement, hoping she wouldn't pay attention, he opened the device and sent a quick text message to Shanna. Phoebe at café.

"Yes. For a while." She hunched her shoulders as if the memory was painful. "I didn't stay long because I knew Anna was coming over after the play."

The slight sneer in her tone gave him a clue that Phoebe wasn't a fan of Brady's girlfriend. "Were you hoping Anna and Brady would break up?"

Phoebe ducked her head, hiding behind her purple-streaked jet-black hair. "Can't hurt to hope he'd finally see past the fakeness to her true colors, right? She wasn't that good of an actress."

A shiver of unease slid down his spine. Was it possible their initial love-triangle theory had some merit after all? Both Anna and Phoebe seemed to care for Brady. Had one of them bashed him on the head?

He found himself hoping and praying neither girl was a potential murderer.

"What time did you leave the party?" he asked.

She shrugged and then sneezed again. "Probably around nine-thirty or ten. That's what time Brady thought the play would be over."

The time Brady thought Anna might come? "So Brady was trying to keep the two of you apart?"

She avoided his gaze. "Only to avoid another scene."

"What happened?"

"I was working Friday night—the night before the party—and Brady was at the café working on his article. I sat with him while on break, and of course Anna showed up. She went crazy, yelling and screaming at Brady. My manager came out, threatening to call the cops, so Anna left. Brady went after her."

He winced a little at her resigned tone. "I'm

sure that was difficult for you, considering how much you cared about him."

"A little," she allowed.

He was about to ask another question when a familiar SUV suddenly pulled over to the curb beside them. Despite the no-parking zone, Shanna jumped from the vehicle and approached them.

"Phoebe?" she asked in a rush.

The girl looked taken aback. "What do you want?"

Quinn put his hand on Shanna's arm, trying to warn her to go slow. He hadn't even asked whether or not Phoebe was adopted. "Phoebe, this is my friend, Shanna Dawson. Remember I told you she wanted to ask you a few questions?"

Phoebe took a step back, shaking her head. "Look, I'm done with this scene. I don't know who hurt Brady, and I'm sick. I need to go home. Maybe we can do this some other day, okay?"

"No, wait!" Shanna said urgently. "Please, Phoebe, just give me five minutes?"

The girl with the purple-streaked hair let out a heavy sigh. "Okay, what do you want to know?"

Shanna hesitated and glanced up at him, as if unsure how to proceed. Since he'd established some sort of rapport with her, he asked the question he knew was burning first and foremost in

Shanna's mind. "Phoebe, were you helping Brady with his adoption story?"

Her eyes widened in surprise. "How did you know?"

"Were you adopted, too?" Shanna asked.

"Yes, I was adopted. And Brady did want to include me in his story. I wasn't really that anxious to participate, though. I mean, yeah, Dennis wanted to find his birth mother, but I didn't."

Shanna paled. "You didn't?"

"No. Why would I want to find some woman who didn't want me?" Phoebe asked in a hard tone. "One set of parents constantly fighting was bad enough. I wasn't anxious to add another parent into the mix."

Shanna stared at Phoebe in dismay. From the moment she'd faced the girl, she was convinced Phoebe was Skylar. She was adopted, for one thing, but the big brown eyes and the heart-shaped face bore an eerie resemblance to the age-progression photo of Skylar.

"What if I told you that your mother didn't give you up at birth?" Shanna asked, keeping her voice steady with an effort. "What if I told you that you were kidnapped as a five-year-old child and adopted by someone else illegally?"

Now it was Phoebe's turn to pale, her red nose

standing out starkly against her features. "No. I don't believe you."

"I'm not lying about this. There's an FBI agent working on the case right now. I—we believe you might be my sister, Skylar Dawson."

"I'm not your sister," Phoebe said now, her tone carrying a hint of panic. "My parents told me I was adopted as an infant."

"So you don't remember this?" Shanna pulled out the stuffed elephant triumphantly. "Ellie the elephant was your favorite toy. You took her everywhere with you."

Shanna thought there was a flash of recognition in her sister's eyes, but then Phoebe was shaking her head vehemently. "No, I don't. I'm not listening to any more of your garbage, either. Leave me alone, do you hear me?"

Phoebe spun away and Shanna moved to follow, but Quinn stopped her with a hand on her arm. "Don't," he advised in a low tone. "Give her some time, Shanna."

She watched Phoebe hurry away, heading in the direction of her apartment. "But she's Skylar. She looks just like the age-progression photo I have. I know she's Skylar!"

"It's highly likely," Quinn agreed. "And I'm sure we'll get her fingerprint match to prove it.

But that doesn't mean she's going to welcome you or your parents with open arms, Shanna."

She closed her eyes and ran an unsteady hand through her hair. Quinn was right. Skylar's expression had mirrored that of Dennis Green as he'd waited to be interviewed by Agent Tanner.

She'd found her long-lost sister, but clearly Skylar wasn't interested in the family she'd been taken from fourteen years ago.

"Don't torture yourself over this, Shanna," Quinn said. "You found your sister alive and well. Isn't that what matters most? And given time, she might come around."

"I hope so, Quinn," she murmured. Reaching into her pocket, she pulled out the age-progression photograph and showed it to him. "See what I mean? Once you look past the purple hair and the eyebrow piercing, you can see they're the same person."

"The resemblance is difficult to ignore," Quinn agreed. "So we'll let Agent Tanner know, and he'll take over from here. Who knows, maybe she'll believe someone in authority, like the FBI, rather than the two of us."

She nodded, trying not to be disheartened. Quinn was right, though. God had helped her find Skylar, and there was nothing more she could do to change Skylar's mind about her family.

She'd leave that problem in God's hands, too. *Please, Lord, help Skylar to realize how much we love her, care about her and miss her. Amen.*

"Are you ready to eat?" Quinn asked.

Shanna shook her head. "I'm not hungry, and if you don't mind, I want to see my mom."

"You don't have proof yet that Phoebe is Skylar," he pointed out reasonably.

"I have the proof I need," she said, holding up the age-progression photo. "Did you see the way she looked at the stuffed elephant? Phoebe is Skylar, all right. And my mother deserves to know she's alive."

Quinn looked as if he wanted to argue, but then he stepped back. "Okay, will you call me afterwards?"

"Sure," she replied, somewhat absently. She was glad he wasn't going to try to stop her from doing what she knew in her heart was right. Impulsively, she gave him a quick hug. "See you later."

"Take care," he said, hugging her back.

Smiling for the first time since she'd received his text message, she walked around to get into his SUV.

The ride to her mother's house didn't take long. Her mom had stayed in the house after her parents had split up, and Shanna knew her mother refused to move because she secretly hoped her sister would somehow find her way back home.

Her father hadn't moved far, either; his auto-repair shop was close to the Carlyle University campus.

When she knocked on her mother's front door, she looked surprised to see her. "Shanna, what are you doing here?"

"I found Skylar," she blurted.

Her mother swayed and grabbed the edge of the door for support. "What? Did I hear you correctly? You found Skylar?"

"Yes, Mom. I did. Can we sit down for a minute? I'll tell you the whole story."

Her mother opened the door, and the two of them headed for the kitchen. Glancing around at the house she'd grown up in, she felt the familiar pang of nostalgia.

But this time, there wasn't any guilt. Yes, she should have walked Skylar inside the school building, but her sister's kidnapping wasn't totally her fault. Based on what Agent Tanner had revealed, there was a ring of criminals who preyed on innocent and vulnerable children.

Her mother made a pot of decaf coffee while Shanna filled her in on everything that had happened, from the moment she'd found Skylar's fingerprints at Brady's crime scene to finding and talking to Phoebe Fontaine.

"And you're certain this Phoebe is really Skylar?" her mother asked, cradling her coffee mug in her hand.

"We'll get the fingerprint match to prove it, but based on your age-progression photos and her subtle reaction to Ellie the elephant, I'm sure."

"I can't believe it," her mother murmured. "After all this time, we finally know that Skylar is alive."

"I know, it's nothing short of amazing, isn't it?" Shanna asked. "And now that I've told you, my next stop will be to tell Dad. I know he's mad at me, but surely once he realizes Skylar is alive he'll find a way to forgive me."

"I don't think that's a good idea," her mother said when Shanna stood.

She stared at her mother. "Why not? I've been trying to talk to Dad for a few weeks now, but he wouldn't listen. But he has to listen if I tell him I found Skylar."

"I think Larry will take the news better coming from me," her mother argued.

"But that's the whole point, Mom. I want to mend this ridiculous feud between us. I know Dad blames me for Skylar's kidnapping, but at least

I've avenged some of the wrong I did by finding her."

"You don't understand, Shanna," her mother said, twisting her hands in her lap anxiously. "There's another reason your father won't talk to you."

There was? Shanna slowly sank back into her chair. "What is it, Mom?"

Her mother paused for so long, Shanna feared she wouldn't tell her, but then finally, she raised her tortured gaze. "Early in our marriage, I had an affair. And when I discovered I was pregnant with you, the man I was seeing took off, returning to college a hundred miles away from here. I know what I did was wrong, and the fact that we were having some marriage problems isn't a good excuse. And of course my cheating with another man certainly didn't help. Larry was angry and upset, but after some extensive marriage counseling, we agreed to stay together and try again."

An affair? Her blood turned cold as the knowledge sank deep. "Are you saying what I think you're saying?" she hoarsely asked.

Tears filled her mother's eyes. "Yes. I'm sorry Shanna, but you're not Larry's daughter by blood."

Shanna didn't know what to say.

Her mother's voice dropped even lower. "But Skylar is."

FIFTEEN

Shanna stared at her mother in horror. She wasn't her father's biological daughter? Skylar was?

No wonder Skylar looked so much like her father and Shanna didn't.

And that bit of news certainly explained why he'd been so bitterly angry, blaming her for Skylar's kidnapping.

Memories from the past swirled in her mind. The way her father had doted on Skylar from the moment her baby sister was born. The way he'd gone all out for Skylar's birthday, hiring a clown and even offering baby elephant rides because elephants were Skylar's favorite animal.

She hadn't been jealous of her sister, at least not that she remembered. But maybe subconsciously? No, she refused to believe she'd let Skylar go into her kindergarten class alone because subconsciously she wanted something to happen.

Please God, help me make sense of this. Please?

"Forgive me, Shanna," her mother cried, tears filling her eyes. "I thought God had forgiven me, but after Skylar's kidnapping, I realized that God was trying to teach me a lesson, making me atone for my sins."

"Oh, Mom," Shanna murmured, going over to give her mother a hug and a kiss. "Of course I forgive you. And I'm sure Skylar's kidnapping wasn't God trying to punish you. Everything that happened was a test of your faith to make you stronger."

"Maybe," her mother replied uncertainly, sniffling and then reaching for a tissue to blow her nose. "Larry certainly didn't keep his faith. Instead he turned his back on church, God and me. He moved out and started divorce proceedings. I gave him the divorce because that's what he wanted, but deep down, I consider myself still married to him. I keep hoping that someday we'll be a family once again...."

To hear her mother admit that she still hoped for a reconciliation with her father—Skylar's father, rather—was almost as surprising as finding out she wasn't her father's daughter. "Oh, Mom, I'm sorry. So sorry. Skylar's kidnapping was my fault, and you've suffered so much as a result."

"No, Shanna. Don't say that! Skylar's kidnapping was not your fault. I told you that back then, and I firmly believe it now. If it's anyone's fault, it's mine. I could have taken Skylar to her first day of kindergarten. But instead I left the job to you. And Larry constantly reminded me of that bad decision over and over again."

"Maybe it's not either of our faults," Shanna pointed out, giving her mother another hug before going back to her seat. "Bad people kidnapped small children to make money through illegal adoptions. We couldn't know that they'd targeted Skylar. And let's look on the bright side. God brought Skylar back to us, so we have a lot to be thankful for."

"You're right, Shanna."

"And now we can tell Dad, er Larry, that Skylar has been found. Maybe this is what he needs to let go of the past once and for all."

"I hope so." Her mother tried to smile. "But I think it's best if you let me be the one to tell him the news, okay? I'm not sure he'll listen to you long enough to hear anything you'd tell him."

"Okay." Shanna stared at the scarred wood table, gathering her courage to ask about her real father. "Mom, would you please tell me who my biological father is?"

There was a pause before her mother answered. "His name was Randal Hanson, and he was my high-school sweetheart. Larry and I were married young, too young, and he was gone all the time, working during the day and taking classes at night to finish his associate's degree. I ran into Randal during spring break, when he was home from college."

Randal Hanson. Did he live far away? Shanna knew she had some vacation time coming, and she wondered if it might be a possibility to visit the man who'd fathered her.

"When I discovered I was pregnant, I called Randal in Boston to tell him the news. He panicked because he was already engaged to another woman." Her mother looked as if she might start crying again. "So he told me I was on my own, because he was still going to marry his fiancée at the end of the summer."

"I'm sorry, Mom," she said helplessly. What a horrible situation for both of them.

"Don't be—it's my fault. And, Shanna, before you start making plans to go looking for Randal, you need to know he passed away three years ago from cancer."

Passed away? No! For a moment, a wave of anger overwhelmed her. How dare her mother wait until now to tell her the truth? Waiting until after her biological father died so she could never get to know him? Why hadn't her mother told her all those years ago?

She ground her teeth together. Holding back the scathing words that threatened to spill out was one of the hardest things she'd ever had to do.

"Randal did care for you, Shanna," her mother continued, as if clueless to how angry Shanna was. "In fact, he put money into a college fund when you were born. That's how we paid for your tuition."

She managed to nod, unable to trust her voice, trying to rein in her rioting emotions. At least her biological father had cared enough to help her get a good education. Even though he'd left her mother to fend for herself.

Paying for her college had been nice, but she'd rather have met her biological father in person instead of getting the money.

"Shanna?" Her mother reached over to put a hand on her arm. She managed, just barely, not to shake off her touch.

"I'm fine," she finally said. "It's just—a lot to absorb." No wonder Phoebe had reacted so negatively to the news of her kidnapping. It wasn't easy having your illusions shattered.

"I understand," her mother agreed. "And I'm sorry Larry was so unkind to you."

She shrugged. He'd been bitterly angry, but her

mother's husband hadn't been unkind in a physical way. "At least everything makes sense now." She rose to her feet, anxious to leave before she said something she regretted to her mother. "I have to go, but I'll be in touch soon, okay?"

"Sure, dear." Her mother didn't seem to sense anything was amiss as she headed for the door. "Goodbye, Shanna."

"Bye, Mom." She brushed a quick kiss on her mother's cheek and then bolted out the door, desperate for the safety of Quinn's SUV.

Inside, tears blurred her vision and she swiped them away, wanting nothing more than to get away from here.

Shanna drove without paying much attention to her surroundings, her brain rehashing every shocking bit of news her mother had told her.

Her cell phone rang, and she glanced down at the display. Quinn's name flashed on the screen.

She ignored the call, letting it go to voice mail. She couldn't talk to him. Not right now. Not until she'd come to grips with everything she'd just learned.

Not until she'd found a way to forgive and forget.

Quinn placed a call to Agent Tanner. "I have some news," he said when Tanner picked up the call. "We found Phoebe Fontaine and she admitted she was adopted. Not only that, but when Shanna pulled out a stuffed elephant, Phoebe seemed to recognize it. We believe that Phoebe is Shanna's missing sister, Skylar Dawson."

"Very interesting. Where are you?" Agent Tanner asked abruptly.

"At the Corner Café, near the commons. Why?"

"Stay there. I want to talk to you in person. Give me fifteen minutes."

"All right," Quinn agreed, his curiosity peaked.

He waited in the café, wishing Shanna was with him. He hadn't agreed with her decision to run to her mother's with the news about Phoebe. Not without a firm fingerprint match. And especially not when Phoebe clearly expressed no interest in meeting her birth parents.

"Hey, Murphy," Tanner greeted him as he plopped into a seat beside him in the coffee shop. Quinn was impressed—the FBI agent had gotten there in just over ten minutes. "Interesting turn of events."

"Isn't it?" Quinn didn't need more caffeine, but he sipped his coffee anyway.

Tanner leaned forward eagerly. "I'm going to head over to visit Phoebe as soon as we're finished here. Her prints will prove she's Skylar."

"She wasn't exactly in the mood to cooperate," Quinn said slowly.

"I can get a court order to test her fingerprints. Or we can simply arrest her."

Arrest her? That seemed like overkill. "She'll cooperate," Quinn said. "She was surprised when Shanna confronted her, but given time she'll come around."

Tanner stared for a moment and then changed the subject. "I wanted to talk to you because as I reviewed Brady's notes, I wasn't convinced his murder is actually related to his article. I mean, he just didn't have enough information to make anyone want to kill him to keep him quiet. And how would anyone involved in the New Beginnings Adoption Agency know that he'd stumbled on to them?"

Quinn cradled his coffee and let out a sigh. "You could be right. But then that means we're back to the theory of a love triangle." And now, more than ever, he didn't want Skylar to be a suspect.

"I know. So tell me what information you have regarding Anna Belfast," Agent Tanner asked.

Quinn lifted his brows. "Anna is a sophomore at Carlyle University, just like Brady. She was dating my brother, a fact that was confirmed by several others, including Brady's roommates.

Anna was in the Thespian Club, landing the lead role in *Seven Brides for Seven Brothers*. She's in the theater arts program, and her roommate is Maggie Carson. The two of them work as hostesses at a local restaurant called Olive Grove. That's about all I know. Why?"

"Detective Nelson wanted me to tell you that Anna Belfast was admitted to the hospital two hours ago. Apparently, she was mugged on campus."

The tiny hairs on the back of Quinn's neck stood on end. Mugged? In a flash, he remembered how Shanna had looked lying on the floor of her house, her head bleeding. And now Anna was a victim, too? He shook his head. "That's a strange coincidence."

Tanner let out a harsh laugh. "Murphy, you and I both know there aren't any coincidences. Your first instinct regarding the love triangle was right on target. Unfortunately, Anna Belfast is still unconscious, so we can't question her about what happened. Luckily, the doctor is hopeful she'll recover."

Quinn didn't like where Tanner was going with this new turn of events. "There's no way Phoebe hurt Anna," he protested. "She really was sick—you can't fake a cold. Her nose was red and stuffed up, and she was coughing and sneezing the whole time we talked. Not to mention she's a tiny thing, short and skinny. She wouldn't have the strength to hurt anyone."

Tanner sat back in his seat as if he was enjoying Quinn's discomfort. "Phoebe wasn't working today. In fact, you happened to come across her here when she should have been home resting, right? I'm betting she's stronger than she looks. And how much strength does it take to lift a rock or a brick to hit someone in the back of the head? Phoebe has the motive and the opportunity. Not to mention her fingerprints were found on the rugby trophy."

"No. I don't believe it." Although he couldn't fault Tanner's logic. Hadn't he thought Phoebe might be guilty in the beginning, too? "There were two other unidentified sets of prints on the trophy, and one of those could easily belong to the killer." Knowing Shanna would be crushed at this turn of events, he instinctively pulled out his phone to call her.

"Wait," Tanner said quickly. "Before you make any calls, I have one more piece of interesting information to tell you."

He forced himself to wait, setting his phone carefully on the table before glancing up at Agent Tanner. Suddenly, he wasn't at all certain he liked the guy. "Like what?"

"We did manage to match another set of prints from the rugby trophy."

Quinn braced himself. "You did?"

"Anna Belfast's fingerprints were also found on the trophy from your brother's crime scene." For a moment Tanner's face held distinct satisfaction. "Which makes me believe the three of them—Phoebe, Anna and Brady—were definitely involved. And with Anna in the hospital, Phoebe, aka Skylar Dawson, is the obvious and most logical suspect."

Shanna drove aimlessly for almost twenty minutes before she realized she was close to her home. Feeling safe in Quinn's SUV, she turned down her street and pulled into the driveway. She turned off the engine and sat for a few minutes, trying to pull herself together.

Wishing she'd been given a chance to meet her biological father wasn't going to get her anywhere. Why was she so focused on him? Because she hadn't felt truly loved by the man who'd raised her?

It wasn't as if Randal had stayed around to be a part of her life, either. So what if he'd paid for her college tuition? He'd likely made the gesture out of guilt more than anything. Certainly, he hadn't done it out of love.

And at least now she knew why Larry, the man who'd raised her, hadn't loved her, either.

So why did she feel so betrayed?

She rested her forehead against the steering wheel, trying desperately not to feel so sorry for herself. Self-pity wasn't an admirable trait.

Her mother loved her. God loved her. And Quinn cared about her. Maybe she needed to focus on all the good aspects of her life, instead of whining over missed opportunities.

Help me to forgive and forget, Lord. Give me the strength to move forward with my life, rather than wallowing in the past.

A sense of calmness came over her and she lifted her head, already feeling better. She thought about finding Quinn, but then realized that while she was here at her house, she may as well go inside to get some new clothes since she'd been wearing her current ones for a couple of days. When they'd stopped here earlier for her fingerprint kit, she'd been so excited about finding Phoebe that she'd forgotten to pack more clothes.

Using her key, she unlocked the side door and pushed it open. Remembering how Quinn had gone in first, she waited a moment before walking inside.

The musty smell of a closed house made her

relax. For once, coming home to an empty house was a relief, especially when everything looked exactly like it had earlier in the day. She tossed her purse and keys on the kitchen table and then walked down the hall to her bedroom.

She riffled through her closet, pulling out a couple of casual outfits, but then tossed them aside in favor of long, sweeping skirts, secretly hoping Quinn would like how she looked.

Vain, she thought with a sigh. What was wrong with her? First wallowing in self-pity and then vanity. This wasn't like her at all.

She needed her life to get back to normal. Or at least as normal as it could be now that Skylar had been found.

She gathered two blouses, a sweater, another pair of jeans and a long flowing skirt before heading back to the kitchen. She'd left the overnight bag in the back of Quinn's SUV.

When she saw a bearded man standing in the middle of her kitchen, she let out a scream.

Her stalker!

"Shut up!" he said fiercely, taking a threatening step toward her.

Instinctively, she clamped her mouth shut and took a step back, clutching the clothes tighter to her chest. She stared at the man, looking past the scruffy beard to recognize him. "Dad?" she asked hesitantly.

"Shut up!" he said again, harshly. "I'm not your father."

No, he wasn't. Larry Dawson, the man who'd raised her, wasn't her father. But he was Skylar's father.

"I know," she said calmly, trying to judge the distance between where she stood and the front door. Because he was in front of the kitchen door, she didn't have many escape options. She debated whether or not to run back to her bedroom, but it wasn't as if the door had a lock. He'd catch her before she could open a window and escape.

"I told you I'd find you alone," Larry said, stabbing her with a look of pure hatred. "I should have made sure the job was done right the first time."

The first time? So he'd been the one to hit her on the back of the head. And then she smelled the sick scent of his aftershave. She'd never made time to go to the store to figure out the brand.

Stiffening her spine, she tossed the clothes aside and held up her hand beseechingly. "Please don't do this. I have something to tell you. Your daughter, Skylar, is alive."

His expression didn't change one bit. Instead he took another step forward, and she resisted the urge to back away. If she went any farther down the hall, she'd end up trapped.

"Didn't you hear me?" she urgently demanded. "There's no reason to hurt me. I found Skylar! She's alive and I know she's anxious to reunite with you." That last part was a lie, but she didn't think God would mind, given the circumstances.

"I know where Skylar is," Larry said with a sneer. "I know more than you do about her life."

Her mouth dropped open in surprise. He'd found Phoebe and recognized her as Skylar? No, she found that hard to believe.

Larry must have seen the doubt on her features, because he went on. "She goes by the name of Phoebe and works at the Corner Café Coffee Shop. The café is only two blocks from my auto-repair shop. I stumbled upon her over four months ago, and knew the first time I looked into her eyes that she was my daughter. Skylar."

Four months ago? Why hadn't he called the authorities? Because he'd wanted to reunite with her first? And suddenly missing pieces of the puzzle fell into place. "You killed Brady. Because you knew Phoebe—er, Skylar was falling for him."

"That young kid didn't deserve her," Larry said. "She ran back to the coffee shop, crying on my shoulder about how Brady forced her to leave the party because Anna was due to arrive. So I went back to Brady's party and waited for the right moment."

Shanna sucked in a harsh breath. Had he really just admitted to killing Brady? He'd bashed a young man in the back of the head for a daughter who didn't remember him?

"Skylar is never going to be hurt by anyone, ever again," Larry continued. "I'm always going to be there to protect her. Always."

Sensing he was distracted, she took a chance and rushed across the living room, heading for the front door. Her hand clasped the doorknob and she eagerly tugged it open.

But Larry caught her from behind, yanking her painfully backward. She sprawled on the floor, staring with horror at the only father she'd ever known.

"You'll never escape," he said in a low voice, hovering over her. "Never!"

SIXTEEN

Shanna shivered with fear, feeling sick as she realized the man who'd raised her truly hated her enough to kill her.

Dear God, please help me! Save me!

She dug her heels into the carpet and used her elbows to try crawling backward, away from him. If only she'd called Quinn to let him know she was here. The last time she'd been attacked, Quinn's phone calls had saved her. But tonight, her phone was in her purse on the kitchen table. Even if Quinn called her, Larry wouldn't hear the phone. He wouldn't know that Quinn was looking for her.

This time, she was on her own.

A firm hand grabbed her around the ankle, halting her progress. Belatedly, she realized Larry was wearing latex gloves. He must have worn them the night of Brady's murder, too. No wonder he hadn't left fingerprints on the rugby trophy.

"Oh, no. Not this time," he said with a sneer. "This time I'm going to finish the job right."

"Why?" she asked desperately, trying to find something, anything, to use as a weapon against him. At the moment all she had were words. "What point is there in killing me now?"

"I lost my daughter because of you." The wild glint in his eyes convinced her that his thought process was far from lucid. He was clearly lost in a world all his own. "And you couldn't leave me alone, could you?" He mimicked her with a high tone. "Daddy, please let me in. I just want to talk to you. Please, Daddy?"

She swallowed hard, remembering the messages she'd left on his voice mail and how she'd called out to him through his front door. She'd wanted desperately to mend the rift between them.

But that was before she'd discovered the truth. That he'd never loved her because she wasn't his biological daughter.

"I'm sorry. I'll never call you again," she vowed, still trying to instill some logic into his warped brain. "I promise to never call you or contact you again."

"You think it's that easy?" he demanded, his face twisted in a mask of anger. "Now that you've found Phoebe you'll fill her head with all sorts of sisterly notions. No, there's only one way for this to end. Once you're gone, Phoebe will continue to come to me for help the way she has been for the past few months. Her adopted parents don't care—they're losers. They fight all the time and kicked her out when she was eighteen. I'm the one who'll support her. I'm her real father. Her only father. Me!"

With his hand clamped around her ankle, she couldn't crawl backward any further. Desperately, she reached behind and realized she was up against the end table next to her sofa.

"I'll go away and never contact Phoebe—er, Skylar again," she said. "I promise. There's no reason to hurt me."

"You deserve to die for what you did," he muttered. He lifted his hand, a heavy glass picture frame in his latex-gloved grip.

"No!" she cried. She lunged upward and grabbed the cord of the lamp sitting on top of the end table, knocking it down at the same moment he brought the heavy picture frame toward her head. She ducked, and the picture frame whizzed past her ear, hitting her hard on the shoulder.

Pain zinged down her left arm, leaving her impaired. But she was strangely calm as she picked up the lamp with her right arm and swung it at Larry's head. God must have been with her because she hit him square in the face. He howled and reared backward, blood spurting everywhere from his mashed nose.

Without his hand holding her ankle, she was able to scramble to her feet. She held up the lamp, prepared to swing again, when Quinn came barreling through the living room from the kitchen.

"Leave her alone!" he shouted, rushing Larry and tackling him around the waist. The two of them hit the floor with a horrible thud.

"Quinn!" Shanna helplessly watched them roll around on the floor, each vying for the upper hand. Of course Quinn was younger and stronger, so it didn't take long for him to pin Larry down.

Within moments her father gave up the fight.

"Lawrence Dawson, you're under arrest for attempted murder," Quinn said harshly, pulling a pair of handcuffs out of his back pocket. He slapped one of the handcuffs around her father's wrist and then flipped him over so he could cuff the other wrist behind him. "You have the right to remain silent…"

As Quinn went through the rest of the Miranda rights, Shanna closed her eyes and lowered the lamp to the table, suddenly overwhelmed with emotion.

Thank You, Lord. Thank You for sending Quinn. Thank You for sparing my life.

Quinn hauled her father to his feet and then walked him over to a kitchen chair, forcing him to sit down. She followed more slowly as Quinn stepped back, keeping a wary eye on his prisoner.

"He admitted to killing Brady," she said, rubbing her sore shoulder, "because your brother treated Phoebe badly. He recognized Phoebe as Skylar and has established a rapport with her. He's been trying to protect her!"

Quinn's expression darkened, but he nodded. "I shouldn't be surprised. I believe he tried to kill Anna Belfast, too."

Her eyes widened in surprise. "Anna? What happened?"

"She was mugged on campus. She's in the hospital with a concussion and has just started to wake up. I eventually remembered how Anna said some creepy old guy was following her. Once we're able to take her statement, we'll add that violation to the list. Don't worry, he's going to have so many charges filed against him, he'll go to jail for a long time."

The wail of sirens could be heard growing louder and louder. Quinn had obviously called for assistance. "How did you know I was here?" she asked.

He looked at her for a long moment, his expression grim. "I don't honestly know, but when you didn't answer my phone calls, I suspected something was wrong. I thought maybe you were upset after visiting your mother, and if so, the most logical place for you to come would be here." His questioning gaze was full of reproach, and she knew he'd wished she'd called him.

She wished she had, too.

"I'm so glad you came when you did," she murmured, wanting to rush over and hug him.

But the sirens pulled into her driveway, and seconds later four armed cops came in through both doors.

"I have the suspect handcuffed," Quinn said loudly. The officers pulled up short, looking disappointed that their firepower wasn't needed.

Of course, the police wanted a statement from her, so she went through the entire chain of events, from the information she'd learned from her mother to coming home and finding him standing in her kitchen.

When she got to the part where he'd tried to hit her on the head with the heavy glass picture frame, Quinn abruptly stood up and came to stand beside her. He placed a reassuring arm around her shoulders.

"I hit him in the face with the base of the lamp," she explained, leaning on Quinn for strength. "I think I broke his nose."

Quinn muttered something under his breath that sounded like, "He's lucky that's all you broke."

She frowned at him before turning back to the officer. "Quinn came in before I had to hit him again."

The officer looked at Quinn, who took up his side of the story. "I tackled him, cuffed him and read him his rights."

The brevity of Quinn's explanation made her smile. "Quinn arrived just in time."

"Okay, I don't think we need anything else at this time," the officer said, rising to his feet. Two of the other cops had already dragged her father out to the squad car. She was glad because she couldn't bear looking at him and seeing the seething hatred reflected in his eyes.

Quinn walked the cop to the door, and when they were finally alone again, he turned to face her. "Are you sure you're all right?"

She nodded, rolling her shoulder experimentally and trying not to wince at the pain. "I'm fine. Maybe a little stiff and sore, but nothing that a dose of ibuprofen won't fix."

Quinn stared at her for a long moment. "Why didn't you call me?" he finally asked. "I was right about you being upset after visiting your mother, wasn't I?"

She sighed and nodded, feeling foolish. In hindsight, her reasons for coming here alone didn't make much sense. "Yes, I was upset. My mother told me she had an affair. Larry isn't my biological father, and that's why he never forgave me for Skylar's kidnapping. All these years, he's hated me because I was here and Skylar wasn't. It all makes so much more sense now that I know the truth."

"I see." Quinn tucked his hands in his pockets as he came closer. "But that still doesn't explain why you didn't call me."

"I should have called you, Quinn," she said softly. "I was upset with my mother because she'd kept my biological father a secret all this time. And since he died three years ago from cancer, I'll never have the chance to know him. Meet him. See him…"

"Hey, it's okay." Quinn took her hand, gently tugging her to her feet. "Don't cry, Shanna. I'm here for you."

She wrapped her arms around his waist and buried her face in his chest. That he was here for her was amazing. Didn't he realize his brother's death was indirectly her fault? "I know," she said in a low, muffled voice. "It's stupid of me to be so upset. I don't even know that my biological father would have wanted any sort of relationship with me, even if he was still alive. But I was so angry at my mother, even though I knew it was wrong."

Quinn stroked a hand down her back, holding her close. After a few minutes, she lifted her head to gaze up at him. "I'm so sorry, Quinn. Your brother died because of me. Because of Skylar's kidnapping."

"Shanna, don't. That man's actions are not your fault." For an instant his expression turned fierce, but then it was gone. "Just knowing he'll spend the rest of his life in jail is enough for me."

She tried to smile. "God always wants us to forgive those who act out against us, so I will forgive him. But I have to admit, after everything he's done, I'm glad I don't share any of his genes."

Quinn's expression turned grim, and he immediately released her and stepped back. "It's getting late. I should leave."

What? She stared at him, trying to figure out what she'd said wrong. "I feel like I need to apologize. Are you still upset with me? Because your brother was killed by the man who raised me? Or because I didn't call you? I'm sorry, Quinn. Please forgive me."

He turned away, as if he couldn't bear to look at her. "No need to apologize, Shanna. As you said, God always forgives our sins, and I promise I don't hold any sort of grudge against you. But

I really do need to leave." He looked around the kitchen, everywhere but directly at her. "I'm sure you'll be all right alone here now that Larry is in custody."

Quinn was pulling away from her, and Shanna instinctively knew that if she let him go now, she'd lose something infinitely precious.

"Please don't go," she begged. "Talk to me, Quinn. Tell me what's bothering you."

He hunched his shoulders, and she thought he was going to simply walk away until he slowly turned back to face her. Stark regret flickered in his green eyes. "Did I mention my father was a Chicago cop?"

She shook her head. "No. I know your parents are divorced, but you haven't said much about your father."

Quinn let out a harsh laugh. "No, I haven't. Because it's not a pretty story to tell. My parents divorced when I was young, and of course they shared joint custody of me, so I went back and forth between them. But once my mother met James and remarried, she didn't have as much time for me. So I ended up staying with my father for longer and longer periods of time. Soon, I was living with my father full-time."

Shanna couldn't help a flash of anger toward Quinn's mother. What sort of woman abandoned her own child? Especially since she sensed that living full-time with his father hadn't been a good thing for Quinn.

The way he stood in her kitchen, so isolated and alone, made her heart ache. She walked toward him, putting her hand on his arm. "I'm sorry. Sounds like your childhood left a lot to be desired."

"Yeah, you could say that." He paused, and she was glad he didn't pull away from her touch as he continued, "My father drank. A lot. At first he managed to drink only on his days off work, but then he was drinking more often until I knew he was likely drinking on the job. I called his partner and best friend on the force to let him know. Luckily, they took him off the streets before he could hurt anyone."

Thank goodness, Shanna thought.

"But being off the streets only made him drink more. They did their best to get him into a program, and he played along for a while, but he always went back to drinking. And then it was too late. One night I came home from work to find him lying on the bathroom floor in a pool of blood."

She sucked in a harsh breath. "Oh, Quinn."

"The doctor told me he had esophageal varices, distended blood vessels in his esophagus, and one of them blew. He ultimately bled to death. I called 911, but he was gone before the paramedics arrived."

Suddenly, she understood what she'd said wrong. She'd been glad she didn't share Larry's genes, but Quinn certainly shared his father's. "Quinn, listen to me. Just because your father drank too much doesn't mean you'll make the same mistake."

"How do you know?" Quinn challenged. "Being a cop is a high-risk job. Some women can't handle knowing we're constantly in danger. My mother couldn't. And neither could Leslie."

A stab of jealousy speared her heart. "Who's Leslie?"

"No one special," he said quickly. "We dated for a while, that's all. I thought maybe one day our relationship would turn serious, but she couldn't put up with my career so she found herself a nice, safe accountant."

The relief was overwhelming. At least he wasn't still in love with Leslie, who was nuts if she thought some accountant was a better catch than Quinn Murphy.

"Good for Leslie. But I don't want a nice, safe accountant," she said boldly. He visibly reacted to her statement, throwing his shoulders back and straightening his spine. "There's nothing wrong with your chosen career, Quinn. I work in law enforcement, too, you know. Granted, as a crime-scene investigator I'm not often in danger, but we are trained for the possibility."

Quinn stared at her for so long she felt her cheeks grow warm. Was he thinking of a graceful way out? Had she been too forward? Too bold?

"Shanna, I know I said this once before, but I don't deserve you."

She let out the breath she'd been subconsciously holding. "Quinn, do you believe in God?"

He looked surprised by the abrupt change of subject. "Yes, Shanna, I do. You've helped show me the way back to my faith. In those long moments when you weren't answering your phone and I knew you were in danger, I prayed over and over for God to keep you safe. I also prayed for the strength to get to you in time."

She smiled, thinking Quinn's timing was just about perfect. "I prayed, too, and obviously God listened to both of our prayers."

"I know I still have a lot to learn," he admitted. "But I was hoping you'd continue to teach me, showing me how to keep my faith."

"Okay, well here's your first lesson. God loves you, Quinn, just as much as He loves me. Just as much as He loves all His children, His followers. He loves you, He watches over you and He answers your prayers, right?"

Quinn nodded hesitantly. "Right."

"So if God loves both of us, how is it that you aren't worthy enough to be with me? Are you implying you know better than God?"

Realization dawned in his eyes. "No, of course not."

She smiled up at him. "Remember when I told you we deserved each other? I really meant that, Quinn. I feel so lucky to have met you. Having you at my side through all this, helping me find my sister, saving me from harm, has meant the world to me."

"Shanna," he murmured, lifting one hand and tucking a stray lock of hair behind her ear. She turned her cheek so that it rested against the palm of his hand. "I'm the lucky one. You have no idea how much I care about you."

"I think I do have an idea. Because I feel the same way, Quinn," she said simply. "And I'm hoping that even though we've solved your brother's murder and found Skylar, you'll still be a part of my life."

"I want that, too, Shanna." Quinn's voice was low, husky. "More than you'll ever know. But

I'm afraid. What if I change into the man my father was?"

"I suppose anything is possible," she said, although she couldn't imagine Quinn ever doing that. "But let me ask you, did your father believe in God? Did he live his faith every day? Did he pray for help with his illness?"

"No." Quinn's expression lit up with hope. "And I'm sure if he had believed in God, his life would have turned out very different."

"Of course it would have," Shanna agreed.

Suddenly, Quinn swept her into his arms, burying his face in her hair. "Shanna, I love you so much!"

Tears of happiness sprang to her eyes and she clutched him close, her heart soaring. "I love you, too, Quinn."

And she knew, deep down, that together they made a great team.

EPILOGUE

One month later

Quinn whistled happily as he walked up Shanna's driveway. The diamond ring he'd purchased burned a hole in his pocket, and he planned to propose marriage tonight. He felt good knowing that he'd found two important pieces of his life that were missing before, God and Shanna.

Before he could knock at the door, Shanna opened it, greeting him with a warm smile. "Hi, Quinn. How was your day?"

"Good," he responded, and he wasn't lying. During the past four weeks, they'd made a pact to share both the good and the bad about their respective jobs. He gave her a quick hug and a warm kiss that went on longer than it should. Finally he huskily asked, "And how was your day?"

"Fair," she murmured with a sigh. "We spent

hours going through the crime scene but didn't find much of anything useful."

"Do you want to talk about it?" he asked, dropping his arms and taking a step back so he could breathe properly. Shanna's scent tended to cloud his brain. The sooner she married him, the better.

"No, it's fine." Shanna smiled as she headed into the kitchen. "I hope you like pot roast, because that's what we're having for dinner."

He'd tried to tell her she didn't need to cook for him, but she'd insisted. Watching her work in the kitchen, he decided not to wait until after dinner. "I love pot roast, but will you come and sit in the living room for a minute?"

She flashed him a concerned look, but did as he asked. "Quinn, is something wrong?"

Her worry made him smile. "No, everything is just right." Once she was seated on the sofa, he went down on one knee and took her hand in his. "Shanna, I love you. I thank God every day for bringing you into my life. Would you please marry me?"

Her eyes rounded, and her mouth dropped open in shock when he presented her with the simple diamond ring. "Oh, Quinn! Yes! Yes, of course I'll marry you! I love you, too."

She leaped off the sofa and he stood just in time to catch her as she threw herself into his arms. He kissed her again, reveling in the moment. "Soon, Shanna. Marry me soon," he whispered.

"I will," she promised, her eyes bright with tears.

The doorbell rang, interrupting their special moment. Shanna scowled. "I hope that's not a salesman," she muttered. He was proud of the way she looked through the window first, before opening the door.

"Phoebe!" Shanna exclaimed, opening the door wide. "Come on in."

"Uh, hi," Phoebe said nervously. Quinn noticed that the purple streaks in her hair had been dyed back to match her natural color, although the eyebrow ring remained. "I—uh—is this a bad time?"

"No, of course not." Shanna darted a warning glance in his direction as she quickly closed the door behind Phoebe. "Please come in. You remember Quinn, right?" When Phoebe nodded, Shanna continued. "How are you?"

"Fine." Phoebe looked distinctly uncomfortable, and Quinn was about to make himself scarce when she suddenly said, "I remember Ellie the elephant."

Shanna's eyes softened and filled once again with tears. "I'm so glad to hear that."

Phoebe went on, as if she needed to get everything off her chest. "I remember Ellie the elephant and I remember the night I had a nightmare and you rubbed my back, talking to me until I fell back asleep."

"Yes, I remember that, too," Shanna whispered. "Oh, Skylar—I mean, Phoebe. I missed you so much when you were gone."

"I'm sorry I didn't remember you sooner," Phoebe said urgently. "But if it makes you feel better, I didn't remember my father, either. All those weeks he came into the café to talk to me, I just thought he was a lonely old man."

Quinn had wondered how Phoebe had taken the news of her father's arrest. "You're not to blame for his actions, Phoebe," he said quickly.

Phoebe sent him a grateful smile before turning back to Shanna. "Agent Tanner has questioned me twice, but I just don't remember anything about the kidnapping. I guess I subconsciously blocked those moments from my mind."

"Please don't worry about it." Shanna jumped up and went over to kneel before her sister. "I'm just so glad you're alive. And healthy. That's all that matters."

"You need to know I won't ever be Skylar again," Phoebe said slowly. "I've been Phoebe too long."

"That's okay. I like the name Phoebe," Shanna said reassuringly. "It suits you."

There was an awkward silence, as if neither knew what else to say. "Phoebe, Shanna never stopped looking for you," Quinn said. "And if she hadn't kept the information from her ongoing investigation, we never would have found you."

"Thanks, Shanna." Phoebe abruptly threw her arms around Shanna in an exuberant hug. "Thanks for never giving up on me."

"Never," Shanna murmured.

"I hope we can be friends," Phoebe said, releasing Shanna and wiping away her tears. "I'm still getting used to all this, but I want us to be friends."

"Of course we can," Shanna agreed. "I'll always be here for you, Phoebe. No matter what."

Quinn caught Shanna's gaze and smiled at her, silently thrilled to see the two sisters united at last.

His family.

* * * * *

Dear Reader,

I've always been fascinated by the forensic work of crime-scene investigators. Science was my favorite subject in college, and I'm impressed at how tiny microscopic details can assist in capturing the bad guys. As a result, I decided to make CSI work the focus of my next few stories.

Shanna Dawson carries a secret guilt—she knows it's her fault her younger sister was kidnapped fourteen years ago. Shanna believes Skylar is likely dead, even though the FBI has never found her, and becomes a CSI investigator to help bring other victims the closure she'd never have.

Campus police officer Quinn Murphy is no stranger to guilt, especially when his younger half brother is murdered at a college party. When Shanna's missing sister's fingerprints show up at Quinn's brother's crime scene, he decides Shanna's sister is the missing link to his brother's murderer.

Past secrets, guilt, love and faith are the main themes in *Proof of Life*. I hope you enjoy Shanna and Quinn's story. I'm always thrilled to hear from my readers, and I can be reached through my website at www.laurascottbooks.com.

Yours in faith,
Laura Scott

Questions for Discussion

1. In the beginning of the story, Shanna feels a lot of guilt related to her younger sister's kidnapping. Have you struggled with guilt in the past? If so, how did you get past it?

2. Early in the story we see that Quinn has a strained relationship with his mother. Have you felt estranged from a family member? If so, how did you mend your broken relationship?

3. When Shanna discovers her kidnapped sister's fingerprints at the crime scene, she rediscovers her faith in God. Please discuss a time when you may have let your faith drift away, only to renew it after a significant event.

4. Quinn starts to feel protective of Shanna after she's attacked by her stalker. He's obviously torn between protecting Shanna and finding his brother's murderer. Describe a time when you were torn between two opposing priorities and how you managed to cope.

5. Shanna and Quinn both come from broken families, and each of them feels guilty for the

role they've played in the splitting up of their parents. Discuss how these similarities helped them build a relationship with each other.

6. At one point in the story, Shanna believes God wants her to show Quinn the way back to his faith. Have you ever helped someone renew their faith? Please discuss.

7. Quinn begins to pray when he realizes Shanna is safe. Discuss a time when the power of prayer helped you through a difficult time.

8. Shanna and Quinn don't immediately get the FBI involved in their investigation because they want to find positive proof first. Did you agree with their decision? Why or why not?

9. Shanna gets very angry with her mother for not telling her the truth about her biological father while he was still alive. Discuss a time you were angry and upset, and how you used your faith to get past those feelings.

10. When Quinn realizes Shanna is in danger, he rushes to her house, instinctively knowing she'd gone there. Discuss a time when you followed your instincts that may have been guided by God.

11. At what point in the story does Quinn fully support his faith in God? Discuss if you've ever had similar experience.

12. At the end of the story, Phoebe admits she remembers her favorite stuffed animal and a brief memory of her sister. Do you have any poignant memories of your childhood? Please share.

LARGER-PRINT BOOKS!

**GET 2 FREE
LARGER-PRINT NOVELS
PLUS 2 FREE
MYSTERY GIFTS**

Love Inspired®
SUSPENSE
RIVETING INSPIRATIONAL ROMANCE

Larger-print novels are now available...

YES! Please send me 2 FREE LARGER-PRINT Love Inspired® Suspense novels and my 2 FREE mystery gifts (gifts are worth about $10). After receiving them, if I don't wish to receive any more books, I can return the shipping statement marked "cancel". If I don't cancel, I will receive 4 brand-new novels every month and be billed just $4.99 per book in the U.S. or $5.49 per book in Canada. That's a saving of at least 23% off the cover price. It's quite a bargain! Shipping and handling is just 50¢ per book in the U.S. and 75¢ per book in Canada.* I understand that accepting the 2 free books and gifts places me under no obligation to buy anything. I can always return a shipment and cancel at any time. Even if I never buy another book, the two free books and gifts are mine to keep forever.

110/310 IDN FEH3

Name	(PLEASE PRINT)	
Address		Apt. #
City	State/Prov.	Zip/Postal Code

Signature (if under 18, a parent or guardian must sign)

Mail to the **Reader Service:**
IN U.S.A.: P.O. Box 1867, Buffalo, NY 14240-1867
IN CANADA: P.O. Box 609, Fort Erie, Ontario L2A 5X3

Not valid for current subscribers to Love Inspired Suspense larger-print books.

**Are you a current subscriber to Love Inspired Suspense books
and want to receive the larger-print edition?
Call 1-800-873-8635 or visit www.ReaderService.com.**

* Terms and prices subject to change without notice. Prices do not include applicable taxes. Sales tax applicable in N.Y. Canadian residents will be charged applicable taxes. Offer not valid in Quebec. This offer is limited to one order per household. All orders subject to credit approval. Credit or debit balances in a customer's account(s) may be offset by any other outstanding balance owed by or to the customer. Please allow 4 to 6 weeks for delivery. Offer available while quantities last.

Your Privacy—The Reader Service is committed to protecting your privacy. Our Privacy Policy is available online at www.ReaderService.com or upon request from the Reader Service.

We make a portion of our mailing list available to reputable third parties that offer products we believe may interest you. If you prefer that we not exchange your name with third parties, or if you wish to clarify or modify your communication preferences, please visit us at www.ReaderService.com/consumerschoice or write to us at Reader Service Preference Service, P.O. Box 9062, Buffalo, NY 14269. Include your complete name and address.

LISUSLP11B

LARGER-PRINT BOOKS!

GET 2 FREE
LARGER-PRINT NOVELS
PLUS 2 FREE
MYSTERY GIFTS

Love Inspired®

Larger-print novels are now available...

LILPI1B